"Who is it?" Dakota asked.

"It's just me, baby. You left something in my truck," Nick said. He sounded quite amused.

She opened the door and held out her hand to take whatever she'd left behind. "That was thoughtful of you. What did I leave?"

She was surprised when Nick entered the apartment, and even more surprised by the unmistakable look of appreciation in his eyes. "I haven't seen legs like that in a long time," he said as his eyes traveled over her frame.

Dakota realized she was indeed exposing a lot of leg in her skimpy sleepwear. Nick was looking at her as if she was a big bowl of peach cobbler or something equally delectable.

"Um, excuse me, I'll be right back," she mumbled as she turned to go back to the bedroom for some jeans and a shirt.

Nick was too quick for her, though. He deftly stepped in front of her to block her way, those maddening eyes of his twinkling as he gave her a smile that could melt steel.

"What's your hurry, baby?"

Books by Melanie Schuster

Kimani Romance

Working Man

Kimani Arabesque

Lucky in Love
Candlelight and You
Until the End of Time
My One and Only Love
Let it Be Me
A Merry Little Christmas
Something to Talk About
A Fool for You
Chain of Fools
The Closer I Get to You

MELANIE SCHUSTER

started reading when she was four, and believes that's why she's a writer today. She was always fascinated with books and loved telling stories. From the time she was very small she wanted to be a writer. She fell in love with romances when she began reading the ones her mother would bring home. She would go to any store that sold paperbacks and load up! When she had a spare moment she was reading.

Melanie loves romance because it's always so hopeful. Despite the harsh realities of life, romance always brings to mind the wonderful, exciting adventure of falling in love and meeting your soul mate. She believes in love and romance with all her heart. She finds fulfillment in writing stories about compelling couples who find true, lasting love in the face of all the obstacles out there. She hopes all her readers find their own true love. If they've already been lucky enough to find it, she hopes they never forget what it felt like to fall in love.

WORKING
MAN

MELANIE
SCHUSTER

To the wonderful women and two good-looking men of my online group. Through the darkest days you were there for me, when there is cause to celebrate, you're there for me, and when prayer is needed you're always there. I wish I had enough room to name you all, but you know who you are. Thanks for the laughter, the friendship, the spiritual support and all the love.

And a special thank-you to Kim Patrice Tookas.
She knows why!

 KIMANI PRESS™

ISBN-13: 978-0-373-86025-8
ISBN-10: 0-373-86025-0

WORKING MAN

Copyright © 2007 by Melanie Schuster

www.kimanipress.com

Printed in U.S.A.

Dear Reader,

I want to thank you for buying *Working Man*. I loved writing it, mostly because it's very different from anything I've done in the past. Opposites can and do attract, but can they stay together despite the odds? That's a main part of what *Working Man* is all about.

Self-love and acceptance are another big part of this story. Sometimes you have to take a step back from the person you think you want to be and look long and hard at the person you are. You might not be a size two, or have hair down to your waist, or have a figure that Beyoncé might envy, but that doesn't mean you're not lovely and worthy of being loved. I once read the following quote from an interview: "I'm not everybody's cup of tea, but I might be somebody's glass of champagne." And that's how I feel about me! Maybe I'm not an icon, but there are going to be some folks who like me just the way I am.

Dakota is Nick's magnum of Moët, but it takes her a minute to realize it. Don't let other people's perceptions hold you back. Whatever you want out of life, go for it! Life is too short to let doubt creep in and block your happiness. Embrace yourself first and see what wonderful things can result when you learn to love you.

Stay blessed!

Melanie

I Chronicles 4:10

Melanieauthor@aol.com

Chapter 1

Dakota took a look at her reflection in the rearview mirror and cringed. "Good googa-moo, I look like the Queen of the Undead," she said with a sigh. And it was true, although she had a good reason. Driving from Washington, D.C., to Chicago all by herself was a daunting task, especially since she was the sole driver of an SUV crammed full of books, clothes and a computer as well as a truly crabby cat. The cat, a large vain Somali female with big green eyes, let out a low yowl to remind Dakota how much she disliked car travel.

"Cha-Cha, I've heard it all before so please put a lid on it. We're here, okay? I just have to stop to get gas and we can be on our way home, all right?"

"Rrrrrowrrr!" Cha-Cha's response seemed disdainful at best, something that actually stung Dakota.

"You're a mean ol' critter, you know that? I just happen to be a very well-known writer and you should treat me with some respect, you hairy little snot. How do you think I pay for all that gourmet cat food and Evian water you consume? You'd better be nice to me or you'll find yourself eating dry kibble from now on."

As she often did, Cha-Cha seemed to understand exactly what Dakota was saying. She looked rather put out but clamped her jaws shut and curled up in her carrier while she feigned sleep. Dakota brightened as she saw a gas station that looked new and clean and, furthermore, boasted a mini-mart. She pulled up to a pump and got out of the car, gratefully stretching. She looked down at her wrinkled jeans and sighed. Nothing to be done about it now; she looked like a bag of rumpled laundry. She filled her tank with premium, muttering under her breath at the obscene total, and then went inside to pay for the gas and use the ladies'

room. It was all she could do to keep from screaming when she saw how really bad she looked. She
wasn't a vain woman, but she always liked to look
her best, and today she was far off the mark. Way
far off.

Her long black hair had gone wild from
blowing in the breeze as she rode with the
windows down much of the way. It was now a
mass of wild ringlets à la early Chaka Khan. She
didn't have on a speck of makeup, although her
classic features looked perfectly fine without it.
She was wearing a pair of boot-cut jeans, her
favorite Nike Shox, a pinstriped cotton shirt that
bore the evidence of the hotdog she'd consumed
earlier and worst of all, she didn't have on a drop
of perfume. Dakota loved smelling good and if she
wasn't mistaken, she now smelled like super
premium gasoline as she always managed to get a
drop or two on herself whenever she filled up her
car, which is why she'd usually pay for full
service.

Rummaging in her tote bag, she unearthed a
huge blue-and-white batik cotton scarf she'd
bought years and years ago on sale at Neiman
Marcus. It had come to her rescue many times

before and it wasn't going to fail her now. Folding it crossways until it was about three inches wide, she tied it on like a headband and sighed at the result. With her big gold hoop earrings, her headband gave her a rather Bohemian air if one didn't look too closely at the wrinkled shirt and the ketchup stain. "Aw, who am I trying to kid? I look like I just got off the bus from a six-month stint at a women's correctional facility," she said, putting her chic little glasses back on her slender nose. "It's a good thing I'm going straight to my place and no one will see me."

Casting a last look over her shoulder she groaned as she beheld the bane of her existence, her generous bottom. If she could just get rid of her big boobs and her equally big butt, she might have a passable figure, but it wasn't happening, at least not today. She left the ladies' room, paid for a bottle of Evian to share with Cha-Cha and strolled back to her pride and joy, her new Chevy HHR.

Her forehead puckered in anxiety as she got behind the steering wheel and stared at the map she'd downloaded from MapQuest. Map-reading was not one of her favorite things, so she concentrated on the page intently. Setting the creased paper aside, she put her vehicle in Reverse and turned to exit the station. She was waiting for a space to open up so she could merge into traffic when a loud thud sounded from the rear. The noise was accompanied by a jolt that shook her hard and sent Cha-Cha into a frenzy. She put the car in Park and turned it off while she collected herself. She was breathing hard with her hand over her bosom when suddenly a shadow crossed her. A deep voice asked if she was all right.

Dakota frowned. Her heart was still pounding and some bozo had the nerve to ask if she was all right. She took a deep breath and was trying to summon a polite answer when the voice sounded again.

"Hey, you in there? Are you okay or what?" The voice was still deep, but its owner sounded impatient. She ignored him while she shushed Cha-Cha, making sure her kitty wasn't hurt.

"It's okay, baby. Some big ape just smashed us up, but we're fine," she soothed, hoping it was the truth. With her heart still pounding and little pinpricks of fear still jolting her, Dakota unhooked her seatbelt and unlocked her door. She turned sideways to exit the car, but her legs refused to support her. Suddenly a strong male hand reached down to help her and practically lifted her out of the vehicle. His muscular arms supported her for a long moment while she tried to gather her wits about her.

"I asked if you were all right. Can you hear me?"

The voice sounded even more impatient, which made Dakota's temper flare up. "How do you think I am, considering the fact that you just slammed into the back of my car? Can you give me a minute to catch my breath?" she asked without a hint of her normal graciousness.

She glared at the man and found herself looking into his chest. She had to angle her head up to get a look at his face, which was obscured by his baseball cap and a pair of Cazal sunglasses. He was tall, too tall for her taste, and had big shoulders that were apparently carved out of the same granite as his big hard arms. For some reason this annoyed her even more and she jerked away from his grasp, making an exaggerated show of brushing off her blouse where he'd touched her.

"Look, lady, I'm sorry about what happened,

but it was an accident. I don't think there was much harm done," he offered.

Dakota shoved her glasses up on her nose, a habit she had when she was upset, and right now she was boiling mad. "We'll just let the police be the judge of that, shall we?" Without another word she stalked to the end of her beloved HHR and frowned when she saw that the left taillight was broken and there was a sizeable dent in the rear end. She glanced at his monstrous Cadillac Escalade and made an ugly face when she saw that the behemoth of a vehicle didn't have a scratch on it. *Figures,* she thought viciously. She was about to dial 911 on her cell phone when the stranger spoke again.

"There's no point in calling the cops because this accident happened on private property. They'll tell us to exchange information and go on about our business," he said in what sounded to Dakota like a condescending tone of voice. She was about to say something scathing when she noticed that the driver of the vehicle was a young, gorgeous woman. Slender, fair-skinned with short reddish curls and a look of horror on her face, she was hardly more than a girl and looked much too young for the big hulking man standing next to her.

She abruptly turned and walked to the front of the car where she dug around in her tote bag for her ever-handy notebook and pen. She wrote out her name, address, cell phone number, office number, the name and number of her insurance company and also got out one of her business cards. She thrust them at him and handed him the notebook so he could give her the same information. While he scribbled in the notebook, she cast another unfriendly look at the driver, who was, if she wasn't mistaken, crying. *Lord love a duck,* Dakota thought angrily. *It's bad enough that she's out with a man old enough to be her father, as soon as she does something stupid she starts bawling. Just pathetic.*

She was so busy glaring she didn't see the man offer her the notebook back. "Lady, are you sure you're all right? We can take you to the emergency room or something because you don't look so hot," he said.

Dakota jumped slightly because she'd all but forgotten the man was standing there. She snatched the notebook back and said she was just fine. "I don't need to go anywhere but home, thank you. I expect to hear from your insurance company tomorrow." Without even a nod to him, she turned and got in the car, bending over slightly as she did so, affording him a good look at her voluptuous fanny. She happened to look in the rearview mirror and saw him staring at her with a big smirk on his face. It was all she could do not to back up and run over the big oaf. How dare he laugh at her because she wasn't an anorexic size-zero like the little twit in his truck?

"See, Cha-Cha, that's why I despise pretty men. They always think they have the right to judge women because of how we look. It doesn't matter who we are or what we have to offer, they look at the outside only. Big macho doody head," she muttered.

Cha-cha had heard it all before, chapter and verse. She was still upset about the small collision and was much more interested in getting out of the death trap on wheels her mistress seemed to love so much. "Mrrrroowww," was all she had to say.

"Okay, baby, okay. We'll be at our new house in a little while and I'll cook you a nice little steak, how's that?"

She continued to croon to the cat until Cha-Cha settled down into a nap. But Dakota's mood wasn't so easily gotten over. She was still pretty hot over her welcome to the Windy City. She hadn't been in the city limits for a good ten minutes before she'd got rear-ended and had had to witness the same kind of mess that had caused her engagement to crash and burn. If Chicago was full of the same kind of men as D.C., she didn't think she'd like it here one bit.

Nick Hunter leaned against the driver's side of the Escalade and watched Dakota pull off. He shook his head and rubbed his index finger in the deep groove of the cleft of his chin, something he always did when he was thinking. *That woman sure was mad,* he thought. *And she's fine, too.*

He smiled a lazy secret smile that only he understood. Most men wouldn't agree, but a pretty woman with a hot temper equaled passion in Nick's eyes. A sudden push in his back broke his concentration. The driver's-side door was opening and a long slender leg was emerging. Nick's smile disappeared as he looked at the young woman scrambling to get out.

"Hold it. Where do you think you're going, baby girl? You wanted to learn to drive a stick and that's exactly what you're going to do."

The young woman's face looked even more dismayed and she gave him a fierce frown. "Uncle Nick, why do you insist on calling me that? I'm an adult, in case you hadn't noticed."

Nick ignored her comment as he got back in the passenger seat and fastened his seat belt. "Well, put your narrow *adult* butt back in that seat and let's get going. A little accident isn't the end of the world, Ebony. If you drive a car you have to be prepared for these situations and you can't let yourself fall apart. Close the door and turn on the ignition and let's hit it." He gave her a calm, un-compromising stare and she had no choice but to do as he said.

"If you weren't my favorite uncle, I'd get out of this gas-guzzling monster and walk home," she mumbled.

"Keep testing me and I'll let you," Nick answered with the grin that never failed to melt a female heart.

Ebony ignored him and concentrated on her driving until they reached her parents' house, which took about ten minutes. She parked in the driveway and turned to Nick with a big grin on her face. "I did it! I'll never do it again because it was a trauma from which I may never recover, but I did it!"

"Ebony, it was a fender-bender. A little bump, that's all. Get over it," Nick advised.

"But Uncle Nick, that lady was so mad! And I did smash up the back of her HHR, which looked brand-new. She was so mad at me, I could just feel it." Ebony shuddered at the memory.

"She was mad because she was scared, baby girl. Getting bumped on the rear when you're not expecting it can rattle you pretty good. She was just a little shaken up, that's all."

Ebony's eyes widened and she tilted her head to one side. "You're not just saying that because she was your type, are you?"

Nick cut his eyes at her before opening his door. "And what would you know about my 'type'?" He stepped down and was halfway to the front door of his brother's house before Ebony caught up with him.

"You know what you like, Uncle Nick. You like them tall and thick and curvy and you like a woman with a head on her shoulders and some spunk. You know that's what you like," she said smugly. "Are you going to call her? You have her name, don't you?"

Nick tried to close the door on her as she continued to bait him, but she was too quick for him. "Where's that paper, Uncle Nick? The one with all her information on it?" She spied it in his shirt pocket and snatched it out, unfolding it and making a dramatic show of reading it aloud.

"Her name is Dakota Phillips…" Ebony's face paled and she looked stricken. "Oh God, I smashed into the back of *Dakota Phillips*," she said, with genuine distress in her voice. She collapsed into the nearest chair and covered her face with both hands.

Nick stared down at his niece, who looked as though she'd just committed a major crime. He took off his baseball cap, tossed his sunglasses into it and put it on an end table. "So who is she, baby girl? You're actin' like you ran over Rosa Parks or something."

Plucking the sheet of paper from her nerveless fingers, Nick stepped over his niece's long legs to sit on the sofa. He leaned back and stretched his legs out to watch her performance. Ebony was just

like her mother, intelligent, emotional and
dramatic. Luckily, she was sweet and loving like
his sister-in-law so he indulged her little histrion-
ics because he found them amusing. "Why are
you so upset, Ebony? I keep telling you it was just
a little accident. That's why people have insurance, to protect them when things get out of order
through no fault of their own. I'm getting ready to
call my insurance company right now and her ride
will be fixed in no time. No big deal."

Ebony dropped her hands and found her voice.
"Dakota Phillips happens to be the greatest writer
of true crime stories in the country, Uncle Nick.
She's brilliant. She's beyond brilliant, she's a true
genius! She's won all kinds of awards and prizes
and she even got a genius grant from the National
Endowment of the Arts when she was like,
nineteen or something. All of her books are on the
New York Times bestseller list and three of them
have been made into movies. She's been nomi-
nated for an Oscar for an original screenplay and
she even has a Pulitzer Prize. And I destroyed her
car," Ebony moaned. "She's the whole reason I
decided to major in journalism and I almost killed
the woman!"

Nick looked deeply interested in her babbling. "A Pulitzer Prize, huh? Is that anything like a Heisman Trophy?" he asked innocently.

Ebony made a sound of impatience. "Aww, quit playin'! You know what a Pulitzer is, Uncle Nick. Don't act you don't have a clue. I'm so embarrassed I could die. I've worshipped her for years and what's the first thing I do when I get close enough to tell her how much I admire her work? I crash into her like a class-A fool."

"Who crashed what? Did you do something to my truck?" A deep voice came from the dining room, followed by a man who looked a lot like Nick. It was his brother Paul, and the family resemblance was unmistakable. They were both tall, although Nick had about two inches on Paul. They were both light brown, although Nick was a good bit lighter. They both had curly black hair and chiseled features, but Nick had a deep cleft in his chin that Paul was lacking. And they both had gorgeous eyes, but Paul's were hazel while Nick's were green, a true, clear green that was mesmerizing, according to the many women who were attracted to him.

Paul looked from his daughter to his brother

and back again, repeating his question. "Did you wreck my truck?"

"Daddy, your precious truck is in the garage. Uncle Nick was teaching me to drive his stick and I crashed into the back of this poor woman's car and now my life is ruined."

"Oh. Did you wreck his Escalade?" Paul asked with interest.

Nick was laughing at the two of them. Paul was always so calm and grounded and his wife and oldest daughter were so dramatic it was a wonder there was ever any peace in the house, but they all managed to get along just fine. "Man, it was a little bump on the fender but the lady's taillight got broken and there's a dent in the back. Ebony's throwing a fit because it seems like the woman is some big-time writer that she has a thing for. She's acting like it's the end of the world for no reason," he said with amusement.

Paul studied his younger brother for a moment. "She must be fine or you wouldn't be grinning like that."

Nick tried again to look innocent. "She's attractive," he said with a shrug.

Ebony heard her mother's voice and went to get

some real sympathy, seeing that she was getting nowhere with her two favorite men. As she left the room muttering, Paul raised an eyebrow at Nick.

"Okay, man, she's fine as hell," he admitted.

"Big girl?" Paul queried.

"Tall, thick, big juicy booty and a hot temper," Nick answered. "And new in town. Car has D.C. plates on it."

"You plan to see her again?"

Nick's eyes softened as he thought about how hot and sexy she'd looked, all rumpled and angry. "I surely do. And as soon as possible."

At that precise moment, Dakota was standing in the living room of her newly refurbished townhouse. She was staring around the place she had expected to call home and she wasn't happy. Cha-Cha was running around their new abode emitting squeaks of discovery as she explored, but Dakota couldn't move. This wasn't the house she'd contracted for, the one for which she'd paid. This place was a mess.

There was still drywall in the kitchen, the floors hadn't been sanded and finished in the honey oak she'd specified, the countertops and glass-fronted cupboards weren't the quality she'd selected and everywhere she had looked there was evidence of shoddy workmanship. She was so angry she was past tears. She was at the point where she wanted to call her father and ask to borrow one of his hunting rifles, just for a little while. She wanted to find the sleazy developer who'd taken her for a ride and put a few bullets in him where they'd do the most good.

She jumped as her cell phone went off and then frowned deeply as she saw who the caller was. It was her brother Johnny and she had a few words for him.

"So how do you like your new home? Did Bernard do a great job or what?" he asked in a jovial voice.

"Your friend Bernard is a liar and a crook. This place is a mess and I hate it almost as much as I hate you at the moment. You told me this guy was trustworthy and reliable, which is why I went into this deal sight unseen. You told me that he was a good friend of yours as well as being your frat brother and that he'd do an excellent job. And you told me that you'd be checking in with him every time you were in Chicago on business. Well, if you were checking in with him you must have been blindfolded each and every time because anybody with an iota of common sense could see that this place is a dump," she said hotly.

"Obviously, you never set foot in the place, which means that you lied to me. If you didn't want to be bothered with me why didn't you say so? I trusted you, which meant I trusted your sorry friend Bernard Jackson. I can't believe you got me hooked up with someone who's obviously a con artist. How could you do this to me, you…you…"

"Hold on, Dakota, hold it right there," Johnny said hastily. "Are you trying to tell me that Bernard didn't deliver what he promised? I thought he was sending you pictures of his progress and he had a virtual tour of the house online so you could see how things were going," he said in a puzzled voice.

"And I thought I could trust you," she returned angrily. "It seems we were both wrong. He was sending me pictures all right, and there was a nice little virtual tour that I monitored every day. But I don't know where he got the pictures from and I sure don't know what that tour was all about because what he was showing me wasn't this dump. And if you'd done what you promised me you'd do, you would have seen it for yourself. Now the jerk won't answer my phone calls. I went to the office at the address he gave me and it's locked up. What kind of friends do you have, Johnny? And how could you get me involved with a sleazeball like him? When I think of the money I spent on this place…" Her voice finally died off from sheer exhaustion and rage, and she stopped talking because she couldn't trust herself to speak.

If she hadn't been so furious she would have realized how upset her brother was at her words, but she was way beyond listening at that point. It didn't stop Johnny from trying to explain, though.

"Dakota, I apologize, I really do. Bernard is my fraternity brother and I thought I knew him pretty well, but it wasn't like we're best friends or anything. I really was in Chicago a few times for business, and each time I came I made an appointment to see him and to take a look at your place, but every time something came up and he couldn't make it. I admit, that alone should have made me more suspicious, but I would never have expected him to pull a stunt like this. And when I get hold of his ass he'll be sorry he ever tried to mess over my sister, you can believe that."

Dakota was fighting back angry tears and didn't bother to answer him. He continued to probe, though, asking Dakota when she had actually talked to him last, and getting more pertinent information that he hoped would lead to the man's whereabouts. "Look, Cookie," he said comfortingly, "I'll find the buzzard if it's the last thing I do. I don't know what the hell made him think he could con my sister, but I'll take care of him, don't even worry about it."

Hearing him use her childhood nickname almost did her in, but Dakota was no pushover. "Johnny, I appreciate your concern, but you don't have to get involved. You've done more than enough," she said dryly. "I'm not an investigative reporter for nothing. If I can track down a killer who's been hiding out for ten years I can find a lousy, rotten no-good weasel and take care of him my damn self. I'll talk to you later, big brother, I've got to get some stuff out of the car and get settled in for the night."

"Get settled in? You're not spending the night there are you? Why don't you go to a nice hotel until this is all sorted out? That's crazy, Cookie."

"I have my reasons," she replied in an icy-cold voice. "Let it go, Johnny. I can handle my business all by myself. And whatever you do, *don't* tell

Daddy. The last thing I need is him coming to town with a caravan of Teamsters ready to hunt that lousy ferret down and hang him. I want him alive and well for his court date because I'm going to sue him so tough his great-grandchildren will still be paying off his debts." She added a few colorful and profane sentiments before getting off the phone.

Cha-Cha sensed her bad mood and came to sit in her lap. Dakota continued to sit on the floor for a few minutes stroking Cha-Cha's incredible fur, sighing every so often. Then she shook off her angst and told Cha-Cha it was time to get busy. "We've got to get a few things out of the car and get something to eat," she said as she tickled the big cat's chin. "And then we have to get our plan in order. Ol' boy picked the wrong sister to screw around with when he decided to pull this crap on me. Wherever he is, I hope he's getting a good night's sleep because it's the last one he's going to have for a long time."

Chapter 2

Nick meant what he'd told his brother the day before. He intended to see Dakota again and as soon as he could arrange it. He'd called his insurance agent that afternoon and explained the situation, emphasizing that he didn't want her to have to spend a single dime on the repair of her vehicle. "She's new in town, so we need to make sure she gets the best body shop available to take care of her ride. It's a new HHR, but I don't really have that much faith in dealerships. When you talk to her company make some suggestions about repairs, okay?"

Nick's long-time agent was smiling for all she was worth on the other end of the phone. She'd known Nick for years and had never heard so much concern and caring in his voice, but all she said was "Will do, Nick. I'll make sure she gets nothing but the best."

Satisfied that one thing on the agenda was taken care of, Nick moved to the next item. He was going to pay Miss Phillips a visit and he was even bearing flowers, something his sister-in-law had insisted on. He had to laugh when he remembered her exact words. Patsy was as sweet and Southern as she'd been the day Paul had met her some twenty years before and she demanded that the men in her family demonstrate good manners at all times. "Don't go over there empty-handed with a mouth full of gimme and a handful of much obliged. Take her a nice plant or something. It's the least you could do since you and my daughter managed to destroy her car and scare her to death." she'd told him sternly. "And be extra nice to her because I have all her books and I want her to sign them for me."

He was still chuckling when he turned down the street on which Dakota lived, but the mirth died away when he saw where she was living. Another

B. Jackson Production, the sign read. *Oh hell, naw. How in the world did she get caught up with that crook?* He frowned deeply as he surveyed the brick town homes that lined both sides of the street. They looked fine from the outside, but if he knew anything about Bernard Jackson, he knew the interiors of the houses were shoddily put together with substandard materials and work-manship. They were pure-d crap, and every repu-table builder in the state knew it. Bernard Jackson was one of Nick's main business competitors, and to say he couldn't stand the man was a masterpiece of understatement.

After a stint in the army, Nick had returned to Chicago and started his own construction company. He was a master contractor and builder, and had parlayed his expertise into a building firm with an impeccable reputation for expert work. Nick was into land development and real estate as well as residential and commercial building and he'd worked long and hard to make himself into one of the most respected men in the business. He did it by keeping every promise he ever made, by delivering every project on time and on budget and by working harder than anyone else in his company. He had nothing but contempt for men like Bernard Jackson, fast-talking con artists who won jobs by underbidding and then defrauding their clients by using cheap materials and taking shortcuts. The result was crappy houses that weren't worth a quarter of what the clients ended up paying for them.

He particularly hated Bernard because he was a good-looking guy with a snappy wardrobe and a habit of preying on lonely women who'd worked hard to save enough money to refurbish their homes, or worse yet, who'd saved for years to make their dream of home-ownership come true. Bernard was also known to pay off inspectors and appraisers, so his underhanded practices made him rich, instead of putting him in jail where he belonged. For reasons he couldn't understand, the thought of getting his hands around Bernard Jackson's neck and choking the life out of him was very compelling to Nick at the moment. How a woman who was as smart as Dakota Phillips was supposed to be had got tangled up with that lying, conniving, thieving jerk he had no idea, but there was no way Nick was letting him get away with it.

By the time he pulled up in front of Dakota's

unit, he was hot as a firecracker. He glanced at Dakota's bright-red HHR with the sad rear end and made a mental note to make sure she had transportation while it was being repaired. It didn't occur to him that the body shop would see to that, he just didn't want her to be inconvenienced. He was surprised to see her sitting on the front steps when he got out of his truck. She looked rather like a little lost girl sitting there with her elbows on her knees, staring down at her bare feet. Nice, pretty feet, too, with some kind of pinkish nail polish. No corns, bunions or other unsightly things were visible, which gave him a little thrill. Nick loved a woman with sexy feet. She was sexy all over, with her long curly hair flowing loose over her shoulders. She looked up at him approaching and he was thrown off guard by her look of utter hatred.

"Who the hell are you?" she said in a distinctly unfriendly tone of voice.

Nick kept walking until he was at the foot of the stairs. "I'm Nick Hunter. Remember the truck that bumped into you yesterday?"

Dakota looked blank for a moment and then frowned even more. "Oh yeah, I remember. That was the first of three horrible things that have happened to me since I got to this wretched town. Yes, I remember your girlfriend slamming into me like I was invisible. It was a fun day," she said drolly.

A lesser man would have dropped off the flowers and scrammed, but Nick was too tough for that. He made a motion with his free hand and she actually scooted over to make room for him to sit next to her. "I came to apologize again for my niece's part in the mishap," he said, trying not to emphasize the word *niece*. Before she could react, he asked what the other two things were that had caused her to be upset.

"The second thing was getting here and finding my newly refurbished townhouse is a piece of junk. It's a pile of crap from top to bottom and if I ever get my hands on the so-called builder I'm not going to leave enough pieces for them to bury. I don't know how things are done in Chicago, but there are laws against fraud and misrepresentation in D.C., and when I'm through with that piece of slime he's going to be intimately acquainted with every one of them."

She didn't raise her voice, but the calm, deadly words let him know she meant every single one. This impressed him, almost as much as her perfect complexion and her long silky eyelashes. "Well, that's two things. What's the third?"

Dakota looked at him directly for the first time, her face a mask of weary disgust. "My cat, the lovely Cha-Cha, managed to lock me out of the house. I came outside to get something out of the car and before I realized the car keys were in the house, I heard the door slam shut and a loud click, which meant that girlfriend put her big fat paw right on the lock. So I'm out here with no keys and no cell phone and she's in the house laughing at me."

Nick stared at her for a long moment and tried hard not to laugh, but when he turned to see Cha-Cha sitting on the windowsill looking innocent, he had to. He burst into laughter and surprisingly, Dakota didn't seem to be offended. On the contrary, she shrugged. "Knock yourself out. If it was anyone else but me, I'd be laughing, too. You don't happen to have a cell phone I can use, do you?"

Nick gave her a genuine smile this time and assured her he could do better than that. "Here, these are for you. Peace offering. You don't need a phone, you need a man who knows what to do, and that happens to be me. Be right back," he added as he got up and dusted his pants off before heading for the truck.

Dakota looked at the flowers and despite her miserable day, she smiled. They were beautiful: black-eyed Susans, purple freesias and some other blooms that were shades of pink that looked lovely with the bright yellow and purple petals. She turned to the window and waved them at her naughty cat. "Ha! I got flowers and you got nothing. Serves you right, little wench."

She watched Nick retrieve something from his truck and was amazed that she hadn't noticed how handsome he was. Tall, with creamy skin and a body she knew was hard and muscular from their brief encounter the day before, he was a real treat for the eye, especially now that he wasn't wearing that cap and those sunglasses. All that curly hair and those green eyes, super bone structure and those perfect white teeth…if she were in the market for a man, she would have been knocked off her feet for sure. And the way he'd slipped in the information that the young beauty was his niece was real cute, but it wasn't going to get him any points. The way she was feeling towards the male of the species right now just made him an interesting specimen, nothing more. She had no more interest in him than she would in a statue. Although, when he started walking towards her again she had to admit that he reminded her of a Thomas Blackshear statue come to life—perfect features, rich coloring, undeniable sex appeal and total masculinity. She had to suppress a trembling sensation as she watched him walk. He was just a little bit bowlegged and it was incredibly sexy. *Damn him anyway,* she thought. *Damn all men. They're all critters.*

Nick had returned with a tool belt and a smile. Dakota was trying to look evil, but she was too taken with the sight of his long legs in his neatly pressed jeans and his broad chest covered with a nicely fitting blue T-shirt. Besides, she was curious. "So what are the tools for?"

"I'm going to get your door open and then we're going to have a little talk with your cat. It's not safe for her to be locking you out. Chicago is a big city and I wouldn't want anything to happen to you," he said with a sexy twinkle in his eye.

She could feel her eyes widen at his flirtatious words, but she disciplined her face to stay neutral. Ignoring his flirting, Dakota turned so she could watch him work, sniffing the fresh scent of her bouquet as he took a few small tools out of the belt and went to work. He fiddled around with a small pick, and, in minutes, the door popped open.

"That lock is worthless," he told her. "You're going to want to replace it as soon as possible." He opened the door and held his hand out to help her up. She took the hand he extended to her and tried to get up gracefully, but it wasn't really possible. She suddenly remembered that she was not looking her best, in a pair of gray sweats that were so old they were legitimate antiques and a tattered sweatshirt that had once belonged to her father. Well, there was nothing she could do about it now. She gathered what was left of her dignity and invited him in.

As they crossed the threshold, Cha-Cha leaped from her post in the window and made a dive at Nick's feet. Dakota clicked her tongue in mock disgust. "See how you are? You lock me out looking like a bag lady and then you try to put the moves on the man who rescued me. You're a real piece of work, aren't you?"

Cha-Cha ignored her and concentrated on Nick, wrapping herself around his ankles and purring loudly. "You'll have to excuse her," Dakota told him. "She loves men, especially good-looking ones. She likes the sound of their voices or their smell or the feel of their hands or something." As the cat sniffed Nick's feet, she began to purr loudly until Nick bent down and picked her up, something that surprised Dakota. She hadn't pegged him as a cat lover. He let Cha-Cha twine around his upper arms and nestle in his neck while she emitted a low rumbling noise interspersed with little squeaks of joy. Dakota rolled her eyes at the spectacle and looked around for something to put her flowers in.

She excused herself and went into the kitchen, only to have Nick follow her with his new girl-friend draped over his shoulder. "Thanks for the flowers," she said as she looked around for a vase of some kind. There was nothing to be found but a bottle that had once contained mineral water. Nick surprised her again by taking the bottle from her hand and using his pocket knife to trim off the narrow top of the bottle, leaving an unorthodox but effective vase. She took it from him and looked at it. "Thanks again. That was a good idea," she said with a smile. She turned the water on to fill the impromptu container and jumped when a loud rattling sound came out of the tap, followed by a bang and a gush of nasty-looking brown water. "Well, that's just the cherry on the cake of my day. What else can go wrong with the Amityville horror?"

"You need to have your pipes bled. Whoever put them in should have done that before you moved in," Nick said.

"If I ever meet him, I'll be sure to mention that, right before I blow a hole in his butt," she retorted. Cha-Cha appeared to have changed camps because she looked at Dakota with disinterest before giving Nick's ear a contented little lick.

"You never met your contractor? How did that happen?"

"It's a long, stupid and pathetic story and I'm sure you don't have time to listen to it," she muttered as she looked again at the drywall, the crummy workmanship on the counters and the cheap cabinet fronts. Something occurred to her and she turned her eyes to Nick's. "By the way, what are you doing here anyway? You didn't just run by to pick my lock, so I'm guessing you have another reason for being here."

"Yeah, I do. Or I did. Let me take a look around here for a minute and then we'll talk."

Before Dakota could say another word, he left the kitchen with Cha-Cha clinging to his shoulder. In a few minutes he had toured the whole place, stopping in her bedroom and shaking his head. There was her unmade air mattress, a small lamp, a clock radio and her suitcase, opened to reveal some very pretty and colorful underwear. He stopped walking, causing Dakota, who was right on his heels, to bump into his back. "You spent the night here? You slept on the floor of this place all by yourself?"

The incredulity in his voice grated on Dakota's already frayed nerves. "Yes, I spent the night here. What was I supposed to do, sleep in the car? The movers are on their way here with all my worldly goods and the driver doesn't seem to be answering his cell phone. I have to be here when they arrive," she said, brushing her fantastic hair out of her eyes.

"No, what you had to do is to find someplace to store your stuff until this place gets fixed," Nick contradicted her. "It'll be at least three weeks before this place is ready for you to move into, maybe a month. If your furniture is in here it'll just make it that much harder to get the place done right," he told her as he absentmindedly scratched Cha-Cha's ears. She was practically singing with delight at his touch and it was really annoying Dakota for some reason. She abruptly plucked the cat off her perch and put her on the floor.

"Look, Rick," she began.

"Nick," he corrected her. "My full name is Nicholas DeVaughan Hunter, but everyone calls me Nick."

"Okay, *Nick.*" Normally she would have been embarrassed about forgetting someone's name, but it didn't bother her this time. She was too busy reacting to his take-charge tone of voice. The last thing she wanted or needed was to be bossed around by a stranger. "It's obvious this dump needs something. I'm thinking about a gallon of kerosene and a few matches, but that's not really the answer, tempting as it sounds. The point is, I start a new job on Monday, I don't know a soul in Chicago except my new employer and I have no idea where I'm going to find a reliable contractor to fix this place. I have no idea where the crook who did this to me is and trust me, I'm not going to rest until I find him."

"So what's your point? You need a place to put your stuff until this place is ready, you need a place to stay, and you need the best man in the business to get the job done," Nick told her.

"I think we've already established that," Dakota said dryly. "You wouldn't happen to know where I can get any of these things, would you?"

"Of course, darlin'. There's one man for the job and you're looking at him."

Dakota stared at him suspiciously, thinking that he was teasing her. He looked calmly competent and sincere, as though he meant every word. She opened her mouth to start interrogating him, and to her chagrin a huge growl started in her stomach and charged its way out of her in the noisiest way possible.

"You haven't eaten a thing today, have you? You need some food, baby. I'll go get us something and we can work out all the details while we eat."

He didn't wait for her answer; he just turned and left the room. She and Cha-Cha looked at each other with wide eyes. "Chach, girl, who was that masked man?" she murmured. "What in the world are we getting ourselves into *now?*" Her cat had no answer for her other than a soft purr as she wound her way around Dakota's legs.

An hour later, Dakota was in a much better mood. The first thing she'd done when she heard the door close behind Nick was to dash into the bathroom and take a speedy shower. She put on a little makeup, put on her favorite scented lotion and matching perfume and managed to find a cute outfit, a pair of jeans with flowers embroidered down one leg and a soft-pink top with a deep scoop neck and three-quarter-length sleeves. She thought she looked much better than she had that morning, but she wasn't aware of how sexy she looked or she might have put on something else. Since there was nothing to sit on, she dragged the air mattress downstairs to the living room and put it in the center of the room, smiling as she arranged her flowers nearby. She had put a throw over the mattress and it looked kind of cute, albeit makeshift and Bohemian in the middle of the empty room.

Nick returned rather quickly with two bags of food that smelled wonderful to a starving woman and her hungry cat. "I hope you like soul food," he said. "There's a place not too far from here that has the best food in Chicago."

Dakota smiled the first really genuine smile he'd seen on her pretty face. "I eat plenty of it, how do you think my butt got to be this big?" She was so hungry she didn't even think twice about what she'd just revealed to him, she was too interested in the food. "What did you bring us?"

Cha-Cha was going crazy, walking around Nick's ankles in figure eights and making throaty sounds that signaled extreme hunger. "I brought some fried chicken, potato salad and greens. There's some Crowder peas and cornbread, too. You're gonna like their cornbread, it's just like homemade. Your cat must smell that chicken, she's going nuts," he commented.

"Actually, it's the greens she's after. She's crazy about them," Dakota said as she walked to the kitchen to get Cha-Cha's dish.

Nick admired her figure as she walked away. If soul food was what put that luscious behind on her he was going to make sure she had a steady supply from then on. She looked even prettier than she had earlier and he could tell she'd done a little primping while he was gone. It pleased him to see that she'd made the effort, although she would probably deny that's why she'd done it. She returned to the living room, where the cat was now dancing around in excitement.

"Okay, we need to share with her or we won't be able to eat in peace," Dakota said with a smile. "Which one is mine?" she asked, looking at the bags.

Nick reached into the larger bag and took out two containers. "They're both the same, so help yourself," he said as she took one from him.

He watched with amusement as she put a small portion of greens in the cat's dish. She used the plastic knife and fork to cut it up finely, and then added a small piece of cornbread, which she crumbled over the top. Cha-Cha fell on it as though she hadn't eaten for days, purring loudly while she ate. While Dakota cleaned her hands with a small bottle of antibacterial cleanser, Nick watched the scene in amusement.

"I never saw a cat eat greens in my life," he said, taking the bottle from Dakota and using it on his hands.

"Oh, she loves greens, grits and catfish. If you want to see her really go nuts, bring some chitlins up in here. She'll gank you for them," Dakota said before saying a quick grace and taking her first taste of the deliciously prepared food. "This is sooo wonderful! Thank you so much, Nick."

Nick watched her eat and smiled with satisfaction. She ate daintily but with good appetite and was obviously enjoying every bite. He loved watching a pretty woman tackle a good meal, it was a wholesome and sexy sight that often led to some fantastic after-dinner sex, but he wasn't crazy. He knew better than to put some cheap moves on her so soon. She was a different breed of woman and he could sense it, but it didn't stop him from teasing her as he dug into his own meal.

"What you know about chitlins? You look like the beef Wellington type to me. You don't seem like the type who would eat chitlins or pig's feet or anything real down home," he said between bites.

Dakota rolled her eyes at him. "I could ask you what you know about beef Wellington, which I happen to despise. What do you think you know about me that makes you say something like that? Did you bring anything to drink? I'm not touching that water from the kitchen tap," she said grumpily.

Nick indicated the other bag. "I brought us some sweet tea. And you just seem like the real sophisticated type, you know."

Dakota reached for the bag, took out both tall paper cups and handed him one. She opened the other one and took a long draught before cutting her eyes at Nick.

"You know nothing about me. And I doubt that you'll get to know me much better, so let's just keep out of each other's business, okay? Let's talk about what you think you can do for this house, how about that?"

Cha-Cha was inching her way to Nick, trying for another handout. Nick obliged her with a little piece of chicken before fixing her owner with a long sultry gaze.

Dakota was suddenly uneasy with his scrutiny and looked down to see what he was staring at. "Did I spill something? What are you looking at?"

Those big pretty breasts of yours, he thought, but prudently kept that notion to himself. "I was just thinking about how to get your house in order. Why don't you move in with me until everything is finished?" he asked quietly. He enjoyed the look on her face as she really did spill something; iced tea rolled right down her chin and splashed onto her bosom. As much as he wanted to lean over and lick it off, he didn't miss her next words.

"Are you out of your mind?"

By nightfall, Dakota was fairly confident that the man was in full possession of all his faculties. While they ate their dinner, he'd explained to her that he was in the business and that his crew could get her house up to the proper specifications in short order. He also told her that he owned three storage facilities and that he could have her things stored there until the house was ready to be occupied. By the time they'd finished eating, he'd made a few phone calls, and when the movers arrived, he'd directed them to the storage place, and by the time she'd cleaned up after their meal, he was ready to prove to her that he meant every word of what he'd told her.

He took her to his offices, which were spacious and nicely furnished. He introduced her to his office manager, Leticia Banks, and showed her all his credentials, licenses and letters of thanks from grateful clients. Dakota had been impressed in spite of herself. Leticia, who was plump, pretty and well-dressed, had given her a sly smile.

"You look a little overwhelmed, sugar. Don't worry about a thing, Nick can deliver on anything he says he can do," she assured Dakota. "He'll have you hooked up in no time." She gave Dakota a sunny smile that didn't seem to match the coolly assessing look in her eyes, but Dakota filed that away for later consideration. She was too busy trying to calculate how much more this was going to cost her and she was hoping she wouldn't have to go to her father for additional funds. She had a big chunk of money tied up in the Amityville horror, as she was now calling her house, and she dreaded the thought of more debt. She'd been totally upfront with Nick about it, too.

"Look, I believe you. I think you can do what you say, but I'm worried about the cost," she said earnestly as she sat in the comfortable chair that faced his desk. "I already have a bundle tied up in this situation and I'm not made of money. There's not a money tree in my backyard waiting to be harvested," she said with a sigh.

Nick had turned those mesmerizing eyes of his on hers and didn't crack a smile. "Have I asked you about money? You worry too much, baby. I'm trying to help you out and you're questioning every move I want to make."

Dakota blinked her long lashes at him. If she didn't know any better, she would swear there was something personal in what he said, almost something sexual. She stared back at him and once again she had to suppress a strong physical reaction to the man. Suddenly she remembered how he'd snickered when her big behind was getting back into her car after the accident and as angry as the memory made her, it gave her a kind of reassurance. Whatever he wanted from her had nothing to do with sex, he wasn't attracted to her. For once her extra pounds had come in handy. At least she didn't have to worry about him trying to get with her in return for his favors.

"I apologize for being slightly paranoid," she said in a quiet voice. She shrugged her shoulders and added, "But you're a businessman and a good one, from the looks of your operation. You didn't get that way from giving people handouts and as far as I know, construction work doesn't have a pro bono arrangement."

Nick continued to stare at her for a long moment before answering. "Look, baby, it's commendable for you to be honest about your situation and to be concerned about mine, but I got this, okay? I'll get paid because I'm going after Bernard Jackson myself. And when I'm done with him, he won't be able to do this same number on anybody else. People like Jackson give all black builders and contractors a bad name. You aren't the first woman he's swindled and you won't be the last, unless someone puts a stop to it."

Dakota was captivated by the change in Nick as he spoke. The intensity of his voice and his rising emotions made his voice even deeper and he seemed even more masculine than before, if that were possible. Her response to his firm declaration moved her so that she felt another massive tremor working its way through her body and she had to work hard to control the urge to fan away the heat he generated in her. *Oh, this is bad, this is really bad,* she thought. "You sound very sure of yourself," she told him.

Nick leaned back in his oversized desk chair and linked his fingers behind his head. "I am sure of myself. I know what I can do and nothing comes out of my mouth that I can't back up. That's just the way I am. You'll understand that when you get to know me better," he said with a smile that bordered on cocky.

The smug look on his face was enough to snap Dakota back into her senses. She was about to say something smart when Nick excused himself to answer his phone. She took a good long look at him and had to admit she liked what she saw. He was too tall; she liked men who were about six feet, maybe an inch or two taller. She hated a man who loomed over her; there was something bothersome about it. But he was a handsome man, no question. She knew women in D.C. who'd pay to get a date with a man like Nick. Those cheekbones, that strong chin, that head full of beautiful black hair and especially those green eyes—he could have been a model if it weren't for the fact that he was so broad-shouldered and muscular. Suddenly Nick looked up and caught her staring at him. He gave her a smile that could have melted an iceberg and this time she really shivered.

"Okay, Miss Lady, have I convinced you that I can be trusted? Are you going to allow me to do what I do and get your house in order?"

As if she had no will of her own, Dakota felt her head going up and down as she nodded yes. "But I'll still need a place to stay. Are there any residence hotels nearby? Those executive suite places?"

Nick rose and came around the desk, holding out his hand to her as he did so. "Baby, I told you I've got it all handled. Come with me and I'll show you what I mean."

Lordy, what am I getting myself into now? she thought as she accepted his hand.

As though he could read her thoughts, Nick suddenly pulled her up out of her chair and touched her chin with the fingers of his free hand. "You gotta trust me, baby. I got this. Let's go."

Chapter 3

Dakota was just getting out of the shower when her cell phone went off. She pulled the luxurious towel around her body a little tighter and sat on the edge of the bed to answer it, smiling when she heard her sister Billie's voice.

"So what's going on with you? I've heard some disturbing stories," Billie said with a teasing laugh.

"I see you've been talking to our brother," Dakota said dryly. "That boy can't keep anything to himself." She sighed and tried to get more comfortable on the edge of the huge bed.

"I heard the brownstone you bought turned out to be in the projects and you were sleeping in your car, that's all," Billie said. "Is any of that true?"

"None of it! You and Johnny both need to quit exaggerating. I'm sure he didn't say I was sleeping in my.car," Dakota said impatiently. "You two are so dramatic. I don't know what I'm going to do with you."

Billie had a quick answer for her. "You're going to keep being our favorite sister, that's what. Johnny didn't say anything like that, of course, but he was really pissed about that so-called friend of his. So what happened, exactly?"

"The brownstone is a mess, but I have a builder who's going to get it hooked up. He's also going after the guy who did the number on me, says he's a bum and he's done it to other people, too, mostly women. And I'm not sleeping in my car. I'm staying in a furnished apartment, as a matter of fact." She waited two full beats and then added, "I'm staying in *his* apartment." Her mischievous tone of voice did the trick as all she heard was a loud scream from the other end.

"You're staying with him? Girl, have you lost your reason? No wonder you told Johnny not to tell Daddy! I should tell him myself, you idiot. You don't know this joker from a can of paint and you're staying with him? Are all the hotels in Chicago booked up or something?"

"Ooh, girl, you really need to chill. Look up the word *overreaction* in the dictionary and I'll bet your picture will be there. I said I was staying in his furnished apartment, I didn't say anything about him being here, too. He lives in a house, thank you very much, and he just happens to have several rental properties. This apartment is the last place he lived before moving into his home," Dakota told her.

"Oh." Despite her earlier outburst, her sister sounded a little disappointed that Dakota wasn't cohabiting with a stranger. "Well, fill in the gaps then. Don't keep me in suspense. *Give,* woman. Who is this man, where did you meet him and what makes you believe he's not just another con artist? Johnny feels terrible about it, by the way. He's big-time pissed-off at his so-called friend and he plans to do something about it. But tell all, dear. Inquiring minds need to know. Who is this man?"

"His name is Nick. Nick Hunter. He was

teaching his niece how to drive a stick and she bumped into my rear end yesterday. I got out of the car spittin' nails, you know how I am when I'm tired and cranky, and he's there trying to make sure I'm okay. The next day he came over to bring me flowers to apologize and he saw the poor excuse for construction that louse Bernard Jackson left me. He looked the place over, went to get us something to eat and when he came back, he told me he could get it fixed.

"I didn't believe him at first, but he took me to his offices and showed me all his credentials and introduced me to his staff and he even drove me by some of his projects. He also put my furniture in one of his storage facilities until all the work is finished," she added.

Billie pounced on that bit of info. "He has more than one? Is he a dealer or a booster or something?"

Dakota laughed. "Get your mind out of the ghetto, child. He owns three storage facilities. He has about twenty rental homes and four apartment buildings as well as a bunch of other commercial property. He's a builder, land developer, whatever. He's a legitimate businessman, trust me."

"You looked him up, didn't you? As soon as he turned his back you got on your BlackBerry and you were digging into his past like a gopher, I know you," Billie said with amusement.

"I did not look that man up," Dakota retorted. She let a haughty silence build for about thirty seconds before admitting, "I called Harold and he did it for me."

Harold was one of her best friends. They were both investigative reporters and Harold was one of the fastest and most thorough researchers Dakota knew. When she called him he was more than happy to jump on the Internet and pull up more information than she needed. "He's legit," Harold had informed her. "He's a self-made man, and he's very well-respected. Originally from Georgia, grew up in dire poverty, went into the army and came out with a burning desire to be a black Donald Trump apparently. Anyway, he's considered to be one of the best in his field and he does a lot of community work, putting ex-cons to work, that kind of thing. Donates a lot of money, works with Habitat for Humanity and leaps buildings in a single bound. You can trust him."

Dakota recited some of what Harold had told

her and Billie gave a low whistle. "Whoa, sounds like he's quite the man. Dare I ask what he looks like?

Dakota clicked her tongue in disgust. "He's handsome," she said dully. "Tall, fair-skinned, curly black hair, a body that could stop traffic and a deep voice that sounds like he gargles gravel every morning. He's sexy," she said dispiritedly.

Only her sister would understand why the prospect of working with a drop-dead gorgeous man would make a sane woman sound as depressed as Dakota did at the moment. Billie hastened to offer comfort. "Look honey, just because you were engaged to the world's biggest fool doesn't mean that all men are cut from that particular cloth. Lying, cheating, insincere cloth," she mumbled. In a normal speaking voice she went on. "Just because that jughead did what he did doesn't mean you have to spend the rest of your life distrusting men."

"You've been watching Dr. Keith again, haven't you? Look, I'm just trying to get my house fixed properly. This guy could look like Alfred E. Neumann and I wouldn't care. The fact that I'm on an emotional hiatus which may prove permanent has nothing to do with this man, believe me." Her words sounded a little too emphatic, even to her own ears. "He has green eyes, did I tell you? With long eyelashes." Horrified, she covered her mouth even though no one could see her.

Billie, bless her heart, was trying gamely to change the subject. "So what's the apartment like?"

"Like a pimp's pleasure palace," Dakota said succinctly.

"Quit exaggerating! It doesn't look like that," Billie said with a laugh.

"Oh, yes it does," Dakota said promptly. "This is the tackiest place I've ever seen in my life."

Earlier that day, while he was endeavoring to prove to Dakota that he was worthy of her trust, Nick had taken her over to his brother's house to meet his family. He figured that if she met some sane, down-to-earth people who could vouch for him it would go a long way towards convincing her that he wasn't an ax murderer or something worse. So they went to the house and everything was the very image of an all-American family on a Sunday afternoon. Paul was grilling in the backyard and Patsy, wearing an apron over her church dress, was stirring a big pan of fried corn on the stove. Ebony was putting the finishing touches on a tasty-looking tossed salad which she almost knocked off the table when she looked up to see the person standing next to her uncle.

"Oh my God," she gasped, earning a stern look from her mother.

"What have I told you about taking the Lord's name in vain?" She shook her head and patted her hands dry on a linen towel as she smiled at Dakota. "Come on in, sweetie. I'm Patsy Hunter, Nick's sister-in-law. This is my daughter, Ebony, and she's a little beside herself because she's such a fan of yours. She's read everything you've ever written."

Ebony sat frozen in her chair, nodding her head like a bobble-head doll and then she found her voice. "Miss Phillips, I'm so sorry about yesterday, I really am. I feel really, really awful about it, I do. And I'm probably your biggest fan in the world," she said sincerely. "I'm majoring in journalism because you inspired me so much and I've always wanted to meet you and I really hate that I wrecked your car to do it," she ended with a sad face.

Dakota smiled at the young woman and went to the kitchen table in the center of the large sunny room to take a seat across from her. "That was the nicest apology I've ever gotten, although it was totally unnecessary. Driving a stick isn't the easiest thing in the world to learn and you have nothing to be sorry about. I should apologize to *you* for being such a harpy yesterday. I was just overly tired, although that's no excuse for making you feel bad."

Ebony was beaming so brightly it looked as if her face was going to split. Patsy was smiling, too. She batted her eyes at Nick and said, "Well, this is the sweetest lady you've ever brought over here, Nick. I hope we see a lot more of her."

Nick was leaning against the wall, watching the scene in front of him with amusement. Dakota was trying to control her face, but he knew she'd heard what Patsy had just said. He could have made it easy for her, but he was enjoying the little tableau too much. He liked seeing Dakota off her game for a minute so he could see the real woman behind the mask she wore for the public. She looked pretty and flustered and a little embarrassed and it was cute as hell. It gave him a feeling of power over her and he liked it, liked it a lot for some reason. And when Patsy insisted she stay for dinner, he wasn't the least bit surprised.

Dakota protested, saying she didn't want to impose, and Patsy and Ebony assured her it wasn't an imposition in the least. Paul came in with a tray of grilled chicken and steak that smelled heavenly and in short order they were all sitting around the dining-room table enjoying a lovely meal. Ebony was questioning her about her work and Patsy was hanging on every word while Paul kept looking from Nick to Dakota and trying hard not to laugh. Nick knew he was eating her up with his eyes, but he didn't care. Every so often she'd look at him with her pretty black eyes sparkling like stars and he loved every little sensation that resulted from her glances. For some reason he was comfortable around her, more comfortable than he could remember being in a long time and he enjoyed the feeling immensely.

She seemed to be having a good time, too. She answered all of Ebony and Patsy's questions with genuine interest, and she had some words of advice for Ebony regarding her chosen major. "And I'll help you get an internship next summer," she promised the young woman. Ebony's eyes welled up with happy tears and Dakota, who was seated next to her, squeezed her hand firmly.

"Don't thank me. You may end up hating me before it's over. It won't be easy," she cautioned. "But you'll learn so much it'll be worth it. Nothing beats on-the-job training. And by the way, I'd love to take a look at some of your writing."

Ebony's eyes had widened and she got up from the table, telling Dakota she'd be right back. As she was leaving the room, Dakota glanced at the clock on the wall and told Nick she needed to get back to the brownstone. "I really need to get back and see about my girl. She's been alone way too long and there's no telling what she's gotten into. And I need to feed her, too. She's probably starving by now."

Patsy looked horrified. "You left your child alone at that half-done house?" she sputtered indignantly.

Dakota opened her mouth to explain, but Nick was already taking care of it. "Her 'girl' is her cat, Patsy. This cat is something else," he said. "Her name is Cha-Cha and she looks like a fox. She's kinda red with a big fluffy tail and big ears and big green eyes. She'll follow you around like a dog and if you throw a ball or a stick she'll go fetch it. And she eats greens and cornbread, believe it or not. Miss Cha-Cha is a hot mess," he chuckled.

Patsy's eyes widened and she threw her husband a quick glance before turning to Dakota. "What kind of cat is she?"

"She's a Somali. They're kind of rare, I guess. I'd never seen one until I was doing research for a book about this poor woman who was…well, let's just say she met an untimely demise. Anyway, she was a breeder of Somali cats and her family was so happy that I was writing the truth about what happened to her, they gave me a kitten. She's a handful, but I love her to death. They act kind of like dogs in a way because they're very active and they rip and run through the house a few times every day. They're also very smart and they can get into anything, cupboards, refrigerators, drawers, you name it," she said.

"Yeah and they can lock doors, too. Miss Cha-Cha locked Dakota out of her house today," he said with a sexy smile that was just for Dakota.

"She's a mess, but I still have to feed her. I don't like leaving her alone in a strange place for so long."

Nick agreed it was time to go get Cha-Cha and

take her to her new home. "I'll even stop and get her some soul food on the way."

Dakota smiled and shook her head. "You're going to spoil her. She's already crazy about you and you're just making it worse."

They thanked Patsy and Paul for the meal and Dakota offered again to help clean up. Paul said that's why they had children. "Patsy kept asking me for a dishwasher so I gave her four," he said with a straight face. "The other three are at their aunt's house in Georgia. Good thing, too, or you wouldn't have gotten enough to eat," he added.

Ebony had been in the living room on the phone when the couple left, but when she came into the kitchen she saw her parents laughing. "What's so funny?" she asked.

"Your uncle is smitten," her mother said.

"Oh, I knew that yesterday. She's so pretty, Uncle Nick went for her in a heartbeat."

"You don't get it, Ebony. Your uncle *really* likes this lady," her father said.

"You think so?" Ebony tapped her lower lip thoughtfully. "I'm glad you think so, too, but why do you say that?"

Her parents looked at each other and laughed again. "Because your Uncle Nick hates cats," Patsy told her.

After she and Billie ended their call, Dakota tried to get comfortable on the bed and found that the only was she could do that was to sit in the very center of it. She gazed around the room again, in awe of her surroundings. She hadn't been kidding when she'd told Billie it was the tackiest place she'd ever seen. When Nick had opened the door to the place, she'd almost thought he was playing a joke on her.

They had gotten some dinner for Cha-Cha and gone back to the brownstone where Dakota had given the cat a lecture on her future diet. "You're not going to be eating like this every day, so don't get used to it," she'd told her. "This is a special treat."

While the cat quickly devoured her food, Dakota and Nick had put her few belongings into his truck and soon they were on their way to the apartment he insisted she use. "It's empty and there's no need for you to spend a lot of money for a hotel. Just relax, it'll be fine," he assured her. The building was ten stories high and it was a pleasant surprise to Dakota's eyes. It had been built in the thirties and Nick had rescued the deco-looking structure by gutting the inside and restoring it to its former glory. Everything had been carefully modeled to retain the look of the era in which it had been originally built. He'd used exquisite skill and care in putting the building back together and Dakota was blown away by his ability and taste. She was still complimenting him on his workmanship when they reached the door of the apartment he'd once occupied. He'd thrown the door open with a flourish and it was all she could do to keep her eyes open and her mouth shut when she saw what was on the other side.

The interior of the apartment was nothing like the public areas of the building. There was nothing sleek or classic about the furnishings she beheld, unless someone just had a real jones for classic playa-playa decor. The walls were covered in a hideous royal-blue raw silk and there was a big plush rug in the same color in the middle of the living-room floor. It had the misfortune to be covered in faux zebra stripes, but the bizarre design didn't disguise the fact that the rug, like the wall covering, was expensive. And the hardwood floors were beautiful, she freely admitted that. But the things that were arranged on the floor were awful. There were two floor lamps that looked as if they'd been hacked out of a glacier. They were composed of big, irregular blocks of crystal and they were overly bright to Dakota's eyes, as well as being butt-ugly. The sofa seemed to be a mile long and it was cheetah-printed leather that Nick informed her was hand-painted. There were two chairs that made her want to bite the back of her hand to keep from screaming. They were made of gold velvet and they were shaped like high heels. Not the cheap versions, either, these were the originals that Nick had acquired at a gallery. The whole place was like the living room, full of very expensive tasteless items that made her flesh crawl.

The dining room had a gigantic table made entirely of glass. Not acrylic, the way most tables of that kind were constructed, but real glass. It looked like it weighed a ton and Dakota couldn't imagine trying to consume a meal seated there. The chairs carried out the jungle motif as each one was made of pony-skin dyed to emulate some other poor dead beast. She took one look at the light fixture over the dining-room table and this time she did have to put her hand to her face. She'd never seen anything so repulsive in all her life and she'd spent a lot of time in morgues and at murder scenes. It was made of brightly plated gold fixtures and it had crystal dollar signs all over it. Big ones, little ones, medium-sized ones; they were everywhere. There were also prisms interspersed here and there and they caught the light from the hundreds of halogen bulbs that adorned the garish display and made dancing rainbows all over the mirrored walls.

The room made her so uncomfortable that she just stood there wringing her hands while Cha-Cha leapt from chair to chair making excited noises. It was with great relief that she followed Nick into the bedroom. She didn't even bother to control her face as she beheld the gigantic round bed covered in a red crushed-velvet spread.

"Wow," was all she could say. Despite the pleased look on Nick's face, this was not a complimentary *wow*. On the contrary, Dakota was praying he would leave soon so that the laughter she could feel percolating around her toes wouldn't bubble its way up and out of her. The last thing she wanted to do was hurt her benefactor's feelings, but she could only exercise iron control for so long.

She'd told Billie how hard it had been not to burst into hysterics. "You know I have a problem with inappropriate laughter," she began, only to have Billie interrupt her.

"Why do you think I refuse to sit next to you at weddings, funerals and any church service? I know how you are, something will strike you as being funny and you'll bust out laughing like the proverbial hyena and embarrass the whole family," she said.

"I take issue with that, I know me very well and that's a complete exaggeration," Dakota said with an offended sniff. "But girl, it was all I could do to hold back. He's so proud of this place because he did all the decorating himself and it's just wretched, it really is. Everything is top-drawer and very expensive, but it's so over-the-top it's scary. Even his towels are luxurious," she added, rubbing the one wrapped around her with a grateful palm. "Everything is quite costly, but it looks like some new-money mob boss put the place together. Get this, the bed is *round,*" she said with wonder in her voice.

"You just need to guide the man a little," Billie teased. "He has the wherewithal. He just lacks the knowledge to select a more tasteful environment. So he's got money and he's fine, huh? You may have hit the jackpot, sis."

"Not even close. I'm not his type at all," Dakota said quickly. "I caught him looking at my big ass with an ugly smirk on his face."

"Say what? Look, I'm in Montreal right now but you say the word and I'll be there with a two-by-four in hand. I'll kick his butt for him if he thinks he's gonna disrespect my sister," Billie said with an ominous edge to her voice.

"Child, please. This just makes my life more uncomplicated. This is the first time I've actually been glad to be chunky. I don't have to worry about him putting any moves on me and he can just get the work done and scamper. Case closed."

"Oh." Once again, Billie sounded disappointed that her sister wasn't about to get into something wild and illicit. "For the record, you are not 'chunky.' You've got some curves, woman, curves that most men find irresistible. But, for the sake of argument, what would you do if he did find you to his liking? He sounds mighty tasty to me, despite the error of his ways."

That was what had caused Dakota to get off the phone. What *would* she do if Nick came after her? She felt a hot rush of sensation pool between her legs. Cha-Cha appeared next to her as though she knew what her mistress was thinking.

"Okay, he's fine, I'll grant you that. But there's no need in dwelling on it. I'm just a means to an end for him. I get what I want, he gets what he wants and that's it," she said in a soft voice as she smoothed her favorite body butter from Carol's Daughter all over her body. She had just slipped on her favorite nightie, a short gown in pale-pink cotton, when the doorbell rang. She picked up the matching robe and put it on as she walked to the door. Cha-Cha had taken off in the opposite direction, the little traitor.

Making her voice low and gruff, Dakota said "Who is it?" She could have peered out of the peephole, but she stood to the left of the door in case someone was pointing a gun at her.

"It's just me, baby, you left something in my truck and I thought you might need it," Nick said. He sounded quite amused by her little ruse.

She opened the door and held out her hand to

take whatever she'd left behind. "That was thoughtful of you. What did I leave?"

She was surprised when Nick entered the apartment, and even more surprised by the unmistakable look of appreciation in his eyes. "Damn, you're fine. I knew you were pretty, but you are sho-nuff *fine*. I haven't seen legs like that in a long time," he said as his eyes traveled appreciatively over her frame.

Dakota realized two things at the same time. One was that she was indeed exposing a lot of leg in her skimpy sleepwear, and the other was that Nick was looking at her as though she was a big bowl of peach cobbler or something equally delectable.

"Umm, excuse me, I'll be right back," she mumbled as she turned to go back to the bedroom for some jeans and a shirt. Nick was too quick for her, though.

He deftly stepped in front of her to block her way, those maddening eyes of his twinkling down at her as he gave her a smile that could melt steel. "What's your hurry, baby?"

Chapter 4

Dakota looked up at Nick, who was standing in the foyer with a sexy look in his eyes. And it wasn't just his eyes, either. He just looked sexy all over, something that displeased her very much. He had no business standing there looking that good. His slightly damp curls indicated that he'd also taken a shower and he smelled really good, and that increased her discomfort. He was wearing a thin pullover sweater in a warm shade of tobacco-brown that looked as if it was made out of silk. The color was good with his complexion and his eyes and it made his shoulders look even more masculine. The dreamy color of his eyes was more intense and the way he was looking at Dakota made her feel things she'd she hadn't felt in a long time, maybe ever.

"Why are you here?" she said crossly.

His smile got deeper and more appealing as he held up her makeup bag. It was clear acrylic and her expensive cosmetics could be plainly seen. "I told you, this was in the truck and I thought you might need it. You ladies always seem to have the need to put this stuff on," he drawled. He took a step closer to her and without warning he drew his index finger down her cheek. "You don't need anything in this bag, baby. You look pretty enough without it," he told her, his deep voice washing over her like a summer wind.

Her confusion was plain to see as she stared blankly at him. She couldn't think clearly, but she could feel and what she was feeling was highly inappropriate. Her heart rate increased, her skin grew hot and she had the ridiculous urge to return the favor and see if Nick's skin was as smooth to the touch as it looked. She was trying to say something sarcastic to gain control over the situation when he suddenly leaned down and kissed her. It was just a little kiss, an introductory kiss as it were, but his lips were hot and soft and the brief contact made her sizzle right down to her toes. She felt her body leaning towards his and she realized what she was doing. She jumped away from him in an acrobatic move than would have done Cha-Cha proud and kept moving. This time she got away from him and stalked off to the bedroom.

"I'm going to change. Don't you move from that spot," she said, giving him a hostile look.

She was further annoyed to find out that her hands were shaking so hard she couldn't button her denim shirt. She swore under her breath and tossed the shirt aside, selecting a peach V-necked top instead. After putting on her jeans and straightening the top, she went back into the living room to confront her tormentor. He hadn't listened to her, she noted at once. Instead of standing where she'd left him, he was sitting on that awful sofa and leaning back with his long legs stretched out and Cha-Cha, the traitor, purring loudly as she sniffed his neck. Dakota made a little face at the two of them as she walked to the opposite end of the sofa and sat down.

"I don't think this is going to work out," she snapped.

Nick didn't pretend to misunderstand her. "You're wrong. This is going to work out just fine," he countered.

"All I want from you is the work you promised me, nothing else. Once my house is completed, I'll pay you for any expense you don't recoup from that sleazy dirtbag Jackson and that's the end of it. Period. Nothing else is going to happen with us, so don't get it twisted, okay?"

Nick didn't answer her right away; he was busy enjoying the sight on the end of the sofa. She looked so gorgeous with her unadorned face full of righteous indignation and her arms crossed tightly in front of her. If she knew that her pose made her breasts look even more plump and inviting she would've been even more flustered, but he liked looking at her, though what he wanted was to touch her again. That little taste he'd taken wasn't even a good appetizer. This was one beautiful and sexy woman, and Nick was having a hard time controlling the urges he was feeling. But he was a man who knew how to get what he wanted, all he had to do was bide his time, something that was going to be difficult because he wasn't known for being patient. Finally he answered her question.

"I'm not getting anything twisted, baby. This is a win-win situation. There's no reason I can't put your house in order and get to know you a lot better at the same time," he said while Cha-Cha draped herself around his shoulders and purred in his ear. "It's called multitasking. I'm sure you've heard of it, a smart lady like you."

Dakota could feel the heat rising in parts of her body that had been dormant for some time. Things were getting out of hand and she didn't like it. This was more than she'd bargained for and the possibilities for disaster were numerous, dangerously so. If Nick was just going to put her house in order, as he called it, fine. But if he thought there were going to be some fringe benefits involved, he was out of his mind. And the sooner he knew it, the better.

"Look, Mr. Hunter, I think it's best that we lay down some ground rules. All I'm interested in doing is making my house livable and making a success of my new job. That's all," she said firmly. "I'm not interested in getting involved with anyone, particularly not someone I'm working with. It's completely out of the question. And since I'm not your type anyway, there's nothing more to discuss. I think you should leave now."

Nick let her have her say, and then gently removed the ecstatic cat from his body. He rose to his full height and looked down at her. He moved towards her and she stiffened until he gave her a half smile and extended his hand. "You look tired. Walk me to the door and I'll go," he said.

Dakota stared at his hand and found herself putting hers into it. Ignoring the little tremors surging up her arm at his touch, she allowed him to help her up. She tried to pull away but he exerted a gentle pressure on her fingers and she let him continue to hold her hand until they got to the foyer. She was satisfied that her little lecture had worked until Nick turned around to face her and drew her into his arms. She felt as if she was surrounded by him; his muscular arms held her gently but firmly and the warmth of his body was arousing new sensations in every part of her being. He pulled her even closer and looked deep into her eyes, giving her a chance to react to their closeness. She tilted her head back and allowed herself to sink into the emerald depths of his eyes.

This time the kiss wasn't brief and tender. When their mouths connected the tension burst into pyrotechnics of passion that consumed them both. Nick's lips covered Dakota's and their tongues met in a rhythm that signaled the beginning of a long slow dance. With each stroke of his tongue Nick tightened his arms around Dakota until she was helpless to escape him, although escape was the last thing on her mind. She clung to him, her hands moving up and down his biceps, moving against him urgently to assuage the hot yearning that he was creating in her. His hands were moving over her body just as urgently as he stroked her coveted curves and learned just how soft and sensuous she really was. He was holding her so closely he picked her up, anchoring her against his pelvis as he leaned on the door for support.

Their mouths were moving, their tongues were exploring and their hands were mapping each other's bodies until Nick grasped her behind with both of his large hands. He palmed each of her high, firm buttocks and squeezed as she slid down his body until her bare feet touched the floor again. Their mouths came apart slowly, each one nibbling and sucking on the other's lips as they gradually started to breathe normally. Dakota's long lashes lifted slowly and she looked incredibly sexy. He stood away from the door and kept his hands on her small waist, flexing his long fingers. Her nipples were big and prominent through the thin knit of her top and he couldn't resist cupping her breasts and rubbing those delicious buds with his thumbs.

"I'm going to keep doing that until you see it my way, Dakota. You need to know two things about me. Number one, I make my own rules. And number two, you're my *only* type. You're all the woman I want, baby."

And with that, he bent to her lips and kissed her again before walking out the door.

It was Dakota's turn to lean against the door for support, but her legs were too weak to hold her and she slid down the polished wood until her butt was on the floor. Cha-Cha came to investigate and peered at her, emitting a series of soft purring chirps. Dakota picked her up and sighed. "I don't think we're in Kansas anymore, kid. We're in way over our heads."

* * *

Dakota deliberately pushed the activities of the night before into the darkest recesses of her mind. She'd spent the night tossing and turning on the grossly uncomfortable round bed until she'd fallen asleep, which wasn't much better because she dreamed of Nick. All night long she was tortured by sensuous images of the two of them tangled up in each other's arms, engaging in the kinds of intimate acts that belonged in the pages of some erotic romance. When she awakened she was hot, sweaty and thoroughly embarrassed. She'd never lost control with a man like that in real life and why she had to go there in her dreams with Nick Hunter, of all the men in the world, she had no idea.

She had taken a long and unpleasant shower to get ready for work. It wasn't the bathroom that made the shower uncomfortable; that was actually one of the tamer areas of the apartment. The shower compartment was separate from the bathtub and it had double shower heads and a glass door. The water pressure was perfect and gave her a hard, insistent stream that was just wonderful. Unfortunately, she was still tingling from her steamy dreams of Nick and had to use the coldest water possible to snap out of her reverie and report to her new job looking and acting like a professional.

With the aid of her all-purpose black suit and her never-fail updo, she managed to get to the office looking sophisticated and put together, even though she'd had to take a cab to do it. Her vehicle was drivable, but she wasn't about to risk driving around with a broken taillight and out-of-state plates and license in a strange town. She made a mental note to call a body shop that day and specify that she needed a loaner car. She tried not to let her annoyance about the car situation show on her face while she entered the building that would be her new home away from home.

The *Chicago Herald* was housed in a sleekly modern building with an expensively decorated lobby. There were several long couches, a few chairs and several end tables scattered about. There were also copies of the day's paper placed on the tables. Conspicuous by its absence was the presence of a large-screen television with the Bloomberg News or CNN airing, something that was often seen in the waiting areas of large businesses. Not at the *Chicago Herald*, though. "If you want news you'll have to get it from us" was the not-so-subtle message projected as soon as someone entered the building. Dakota liked it, liked it a lot. One of the reasons she'd accepted the position with the *Herald* was its reputation for being a brilliant organization with a real handle on the role of a newspaper in an electronic world. The *Herald* was able to stay true to its roots while offering features that appealed to the computer-dependent. Dakota was looking forward to the challenge of being a member of the team.

Her new boss was Zane Beauchamp, a tall, aristocratic-looking man with a distinctive walk that was almost a swagger. He was over six feet tall, almost as tall as Nick, as a matter of fact. He dressed like royalty, wearing a custom-tailored suit and handmade shoes, but he wasn't at all snotty, despite his unbelievable good looks. He had a perfect complexion, piercing blue eyes and sandy-blond hair that was expensively and expertly cut. He came down to the lobby to greet Dakota and she was impressed that he would take the time to do so. When she told him so, he brushed aside her praise.

"This is all part of my diabolical plan to make

you so happy here you'll never want to leave," he informed her. "You should be aware that every gesture of seeming goodwill on my part has but a single motive behind it, to make you stay here so you can help increase the circulation," he said with a completely deadpan expression on his face.

Dakota's smile turned into a giggle that she tried to disguise. Zane Beauchamp wasn't anything like she'd expected. Beneath his carefully constructed facade of corporate shark lay a man of warmth and good humor, if she wasn't mistaken. As he personally conducted her around and introduced her to the people with whom she'd be working, Dakota was sure she'd like the *Chicago Herald.*

She met the heads of the editorial department, sports, weather, news, technology, health, business, real estate, classifieds and the lifestyle editor. Despite her obvious connection to the news department, she found several of the editors particularly interesting, especially the ones from business and lifestyles. Brian DuPree was the head of the business department and he came across as smart, savvy and good-humored. Toni Brandon was in charge of the lifestyles department, which included cooking, fashion, home decorating and the like. She was also in charge of covering the so-called society events. Toni was tall and curvy like Dakota, but she didn't seem to be the least self-conscious about it. She had creamy ivory skin, blond hair styled in a fashionable short bob, and fascinating blue eyes with a touch of green. She was a true beauty and if Dakota wasn't a trained observer of human behavior, she would have missed the change in Zane's breathing pattern when he introduced her to Toni.

Toni noticed nothing, however, and was bright and cheerful as she offered to take over Dakota's tour. "That way I can give you the real scoop," she said with a smile. "I can tell you where all the bodies are buried, something the boss is way too politically correct to clue you in on."

"Au contraire," Zane protested. "I'm never correct, politically or otherwise. I'm just clueless. I have no idea what's going on around me on a daily basis, which is why I have to hire the best people. Otherwise this paper would consist largely of comic strips and sports statistics." He straight-ened his very expensive silk tie and said he had a meeting. "I'm leaving you in good hands, Dakota.

Toni is the best and brightest of a very smart bunch of people," he said sincerely. His usual sardonic manner was abandoned for a moment and he gave Toni a look that was unguarded and quite startling in its intensity.

Toni didn't seem to notice a thing, however, and carried on chatting with Dakota about her new workplace. "You can see how tiny my office is," she said, "but there's a method to Zane's madness. He wants to keep us on the floor with the reporters as much as possible and I agree. C'mon, I'll take you to your cubicle. I think it's actually near a window," she added.

As they walked across the huge office, stopping for introductions here and there, Dakota noticed how well Toni was dressed. She too, wore a suit, but hers was a skirt suit instead of the pants version that Dakota was wearing. It had a skirt that stopped above her knees and it flared out audaciously, almost daring a man to look at her healthy legs, which were spectacular. The suit was in a heavenly shade of green with a scoop-necked top in a brilliant blue that looked fabulous with it. Her shoes were the same shade of blue with a green T-strap and a three-inch heel. She looked chic yet powerful and Dakota made up her mind to ask her for a few fashion tips. Obviously it was possible for a woman to look professional and feminine at the same time and it was time she learned how to do it.

They arrived at her cubicle which was nicely located in a corner next to the floor-to-ceiling wall-to-wall window. It provided her with a small amount of privacy and Dakota liked it very much, although she could work anywhere. Plus, she wouldn't really be spending that much time at her desk. Most of her time would be spent in the field investigating. She was looking around her surroundings when Toni announced she was taking her to lunch.

"Zane has a lunch planned for you tomorrow," she told her, "but you and I are going to a fabulous little café today. I guarantee you'll love it."

Touched by the offer, Dakota agreed to go. For some reason her stomach was growling like mad. They were crossing the lobby and had just about reached the door when Dakota heard a familiar voice call her name. He only said it once but the deep timbre of his voice made it sound like a rifle shot. Dakota tried not to jump out of her skin when she turned to see Nick walking towards her. Her first reaction was desire, hot and fierce. This ticked her off, so she tried her best to look annoyed and disinterested, which it was hard to do with him looking like he did. He was wearing a summer-weight gray suit that had to be custom-made, given his height and size. His shirt was crisp and white and his tie was audaciously patterned like a peacock's tail, the brilliant colors bringing out his eyes and making him look even more handsome than usual.

Nick didn't seem to notice her struggle to remain composed, he just started talking. "Give me the keys to your car so I can get it to the body shop. Here's the key to your rental car, it's parked about two blocks from here. It's a gold HHR," he added with that devastating grin of his. "I didn't want you to miss your baby too much while it's gone. It should be ready tomorrow afternoon."

Dakota was finding it rather hard to think clearly and it showed in her first words to Nick. "What are you doing here?" she asked inanely. "My car is at home. I took a cab to work."

He gave her a gentle smile as he took her car key and handed her the rental key. "I'm taking care of you. We forgot to talk about the car situa-

tion yesterday, so I handled it." Suddenly he turned
to Toni, who was watching the scene with amusement. "I'm Nick Hunter," he said.

She held out her hand at once. "I'm Toni
Brandon," she said warmly. "I actually know who
you are, Mr. Hunter, you've had some nice cover-
age in our home section. You do good work," she
praised.

"Aw shucks, you're gonna have me all red in the
face in a minute. Thanks for the kind words, but
I'm going to leave you ladies, I'm about to be late
for a meeting." Without warning he lowered his
head and kissed Dakota lightly on the lips. "See
you later," he murmured.

Toni was suitably impressed by what she'd just
witnessed. "You just got to town and you snagged
one of the most eligible men in the greater
Chicago metropolitan area. I'm impressed,
woman, deeply impressed. If I wasn't happily
engaged I'd be begging you for tips for the single
woman. As it is, I'm just going interrogate you
because I'm nosy as hell," she admitted cheer-
fully. "The café is just around the corner and I
can't wait to hear how you two met."

Dakota stifled a long groan and allowed herself

to be swept away by Toni. She hadn't been in Chicago a good seventy-two hours and her life was getting more and more complicated every minute.

Nick was actually quite pleased with himself after his day's activities. He had taken care of Dakota's car, gotten to his meeting on time and he was now headed to her house with a take-out meal. His office manager, Leticia, had questioned his actions, especially since she'd had to follow him to the dealership to drop off Dakota's car and pick him up after his downtown meeting. She had looked at him in the passenger seat and made a skeptical sound with her tongue. "Looks like somebody is getting awfully involved in somebody else's business," she said tartly.

"Yeah, and it looks like that somebody is *you*," he said in a deceptively mild voice. "You need to keep your eyes on the road and don't worry about things that don't concern you." There was no humor in his words and it was quite obvious he meant every one of them. A lesser woman would have shut up at once, but Leticia had known him for too long not to meddle and she felt compelled to push back.

"I just hope you know what you're doing. She doesn't seem like your type, boss. That's all I'm saying."

Nick mulled over her words as he parked his truck in front of the apartment building. He got out and reached inside for the bags of food that were emitting a delicious odor. He didn't understand all this crap about "types." Dakota had said she wasn't his type and now Leticia was saying the same thing. He was a man, she was a woman and she was attractive to him. End of story. Nick liked to keep things as simple as possible, and he saw no need to clutter up what could be a perfectly nice relationship with a bunch of overthinking. He was laughing to himself as he approached the door of the apartment. "Me Tarzan, you Jane," he muttered. *Okay, maybe it's not that simple, but it's not as complicated as everybody is trying to make it, either,* he thought.

He pressed the buzzer in the door and waited for Dakota's response, which wasn't long in coming. She opened the door and leaned against the doorjamb with her arms crossed over her delightful bosom. She had taken her hair down and put on a pair of jeans, but she still had on the tailored shirt she'd worn earlier. Her feet were bare and the sexy toes he'd noticed the day before were still just as cute. She wasn't in any hurry to let him in, she just gave him a look that wasn't hostile, but it wasn't too friendly either.

"What are you doing here?" she asked.

"I brought you dinner," he told her. "I figured you'd be too tired to cook after your first day at work."

Nick watched her face light up with surprise and gratitude. She tried to cover it up with a stern expression but it was too late. "Thank you, Nick. That was very thoughtful of you," she said finally as she opened the door wide. "Come in, please, and make yourself at home."

He did just that, entering the apartment and taking the bags to the kitchen. The kitchen was bigger than most apartment kitchens and it was fully equipped with the latest and most advanced in culinary technology. He grimaced when he looked at the work island where Dakota had obviously been consuming her evening meal—cottage cheese and raw vegetables. A bottle of spring water and a container of watermelon chunks completed the repast. "Was that all you were going to eat? That's not enough to keep a bird alive," he commented.

"I'm trying to umm, watch my weight," Dakota mumbled.

Nick groaned and reached into the cupboard for plates, which he put on the work island. He also got out a couple of glasses while Dakota got silverware. They were joined by Cha-Cha, who was thrilled to see her man again. Nick greeted her affectionately and even though he'd just washed his hands, he bent and picked her up for a little kitty lovin' before putting her down and washing his hands again.

He and Dakota said grace together and after saying "amen" she looked at him expectantly. "So what did you bring us?"

What he'd brought was a feast from one of his favorite restaurants. "I hope you like Greek food," he said as he opened the containers. The smells of lemon, oregano and thyme filled the room and Dakota beamed with pleasure.

"It just so happens that I love all Mediterranean food, especially Greek." They dined on lemon soup, stuffed grape leaves, souvlaki and rice pilaf, with small homemade pitas that were no bigger than the palm of Nick's hand. And for dessert he'd brought baklava. It looked positively decadent with honey syrup oozing out of each piece, and Dakota looked mightily tempted, but she refused.

"It looks delicious, but no thank you," she said with a tinge of sadness in her voice.

Nick rolled his eyes as he got up and cleared the dishes away. "I'm going to make some coffee. Can you drink coffee this late?"

Dakota said she could. "It actually makes me really relaxed for some reason. I've never had a problem drinking coffee at any hour," she admitted. "I can get those," she protested as Nick began to wash the few dishes they'd used.

"I'm already done," he told her. "Now sit down and get comfortable while I make the coffee. Tell me how your first day went."

He was pleased when she did just that, telling him about the people she'd met, the layout of the offices and her impressions of her new boss. When the coffee was ready they took it into the living room and Dakota curled up on one end of the sofa while Nick turned on the stereo. She teased him, saying it was a good thing one of them could work the thing. "I tried to figure out that remote so I could watch the news but it was hopeless," she said.

"I'll teach you how to work it. It's not that hard." The room was filled with soft music as "Sun Goddess" by Ramsey Lewis and Earth, Wind and Fire began to play.

Dakota's eyes shone with appreciation. "I love this CD. You're into old-school music?"

"Old-school, new-school, jazz, rock, hip-hop, I like it all," Nick said as he reached for a piece of baklava. He took a small bite, then held the piece out to Dakota who looked genuinely anguished before succumbing to a bite. Her eyes closed in bliss and a breathy sound of pleasure escaped her as she licked her lips.

"Nick, that's delicious. Don't tempt me any more," she moaned.

Nick decided it was time to put an end to that line of thought. "You think you have a weight problem, don't you? Well, let me be the first one to tell you that you don't. You look just fine to me. A little on the skinny side, but you got enough for me to hold onto. I don't know why women torture themselves to get thin or stay thin or whatever. Everybody ain't the same size and folks need to get over it, that's all."

Dakota started hearing warning bells in her head. "Are you telling me that you think I'm *skinny?* In my entire life I've never been considered skinny. I've been trying to lose the same twenty-five pounds for about ten years and you're telling me you think I'm skinny?" It suddenly dawned on Dakota what Nick was up to and it infuriated her. "Oh, so this is your game. You think because I'm overweight, I'm easy, is that it? You think if you throw around a few lame compliments I'll just spread my chubby legs for you, right? Well you can forget that, buster, it ain't that kind of party," she said furiously. Her face was flushed and her pulse had picked up momentum from sheer rage. She looked as if she was ready to beat Nick's butt with one hand tied behind her back. Nick didn't take the bait, however.

"Who was it that did the job on you, sweetheart? Did some boyfriend try to tell you to lose weight? Your mama stay on your case because you were getting to be kinda curvy? Your girlfriends tell you what a pretty face you have and why don't you take off a few pounds? What was it that made you think you're not beautiful just like you are?"

The flush in Dakota's face turned into a full-on bright-red blush. Nick was getting really close to the mark, displaying a kind of perception she never would have believed possible from a man like him. She was stammering around for a decent response when he continued.

"You're a beautiful woman, Dakota. Not as smart as I thought you were, but you're still beautiful. If you were as smart as you think you are, you'd know that everybody doesn't want a stick figure for a woman," he said in a quietly mesmerizing voice.

"When I was growing up, there were always two or three girls that were supposed to be so danged fine that all the guys would be fighting over them. I could never figure that out, because while they were fighting over the skinny chicks there were all these pretty big girls with the pretty skin and the pretty round arms and the nice big behinds. All that sweetness going to waste while those fools fought over the scrawny heifers like dogs after a bone," he said, shaking his head.

Dakota didn't notice that he was a lot closer to her than he'd been a few minutes before, but somehow they were sitting next to each other. His arm was around her shoulders and he was angling her face to his so she could better concentrate on what he was saying. "You know what you know and you like what you like," he said firmly. "And I like a woman with something for me to grab and hold onto, something I can feel. I like big legs, soft thighs and a big behind. I like breasts, baby, nice round ones like yours, the kind I can rub and kiss and massage until you come in my arms," he said softly.

At her look of disbelief, Nick chuckled. "Oh yeah, baby, I can do that. I can make you melt, sweetheart, without taking off a stitch of your clothes. When I make love to you, you're going to feel it all over, like you've never felt anything else. You're going to think you're a virgin again when we get to make love the first time. And you're going to love every minute of it, just as much as I will," he promised.

Dakota tried to pull her eyes away from his, but it was impossible. "You sound pretty sure of yourself. What makes you think I'm going to let you put your hands on me? I don't know you from Adam and I'm not trying to get to know you, either," she said in a game attempt to put him in his place. His only answer was to kiss her, a soft gentle kiss that grew into the same kind of heated tempest that had overtaken them the night before. With a deep, shuddering sigh, Dakota put her arms around his neck and arched her body into his, letting the sweet passion take her where it would.

His lips caressed hers, cajoled them and teased them until she opened her lips to receive the luscious tribute of his tongue. Somehow she ended up in his lap and her fingers were tangled in his curly hair as she returned his kisses with a fervor she didn't know she possessed. The licking and sucking and nibbling might have lasted for hours but the tensions that were building wouldn't allow it. Nick had to call a halt to their loving, gently pulling away from her eager mouth and holding her close against his heart until their breathing had slowed a little and he was able to speak. "Now what were you saying about putting my hands on you? You don't seem to mind," he teased her gently.

Dakota put her face in the crook of his neck and inhaled his fragrance while his long, clever fingers massaged her breast through her shirt. "I think I'm supposed to be embarrassed right about now," she murmured. "This is the part where I slap you silly and run out of the room." She did no such thing; she just cuddled closer to him and played with the hair at the nape of his neck with her free hand.

Nick laughed a deep comforting laugh that shook his whole frame. "Well I'm glad you're not acting all shame-faced and girly because you have nothing to be ashamed of. We're going to be together soon, Dakota. I'm not trying to rush you, but I believe in making things real plain. You're going to be mine sooner or later, so you may as well get used to the idea now. I'm not going anywhere, baby, and neither are you."

Dakota rallied the last of her senses and raised her head to issue a protest at his cocky, overly-confident words. Instead, Nick fixed her with a look so warm and tender all she could do was part her lips for another kiss that was as sweet and thoroughly arousing as the first one. She could tell him off in just a minute but right now it didn't make sense to waste a perfectly lovely kiss, she thought as she laced her fingers through his hair again and moaned softly while he continued his tender assault on her breasts with his long fingers. She gasped and her eyes flew open as she discovered that Nick Hunter was indeed a man of his word. He'd made good on his first promise to her and he was right, she hadn't taken off one stitch of clothing. But he really had made her melt into his arms. Her last conscious thought was that Nick Hunter was not only dangerous, he was deadly and if she planned to stay intact she needed to stay far away from him.

But not before they shared one more kiss…

Chapter 5

This time it was Dakota who ended the kiss, delicious as it was. She abruptly pushed Nick away and glared at him. "Looky here, buster. You need to find something else for your mouth to do because you can't go around kissing me every time you take a notion. I told you before, I don't know you from Adam and I'm not about to get involved with you or anyone else," she said hotly.

Her words might have carried more weight if she hadn't been sitting in his lap letting him kiss each of her fingers in turn. He finished kissing her hand and leaned back on the sofa looking quite pleased with himself. "You sure like to hear yourself talk, don't you?"

"Yes, I actually do," she admitted. "Mostly because I make more sense than a lot of people, especially you. We don't know each other at all and we're sitting her pawing each other like a couple of teenagers."

Nick had to exert a mighty effort not to kiss her again. She looked so sexy and adorable that he wanted to pick her up and carry her off to the bedroom, but he knew there'd be hell to pay if he tried it. So he decided to go another way. He removed her from his lap and sat her next to him on the soft cushions and smiled when she scooted away from him. "Okay, so we don't know each other. How do you suggest we remedy that? Since you don't want to be involved with anyone, I figured you wouldn't mind a little happy sex on the side. Getting to know each other implies a relationship, you know. Is that what you want?"

Dakota was relieved when Cha-Cha launched herself onto Nick because it gave her a chance to get her bearings. "You seem pretty fond of the sound of your voice, too," she said as she straightened her rumpled shirt. "And you're rather good at twisting my words. No one said anything about a relationship, I was merely pointing out that I'm not the type to cavort around with men I don't know."

"Glad to hear it," Nick said as he stroked the blissful cat. "I don't like loose women. They'll do anything with anybody and I'm not down for that. I don't think you're whorish or wild, I just think you're cute as hell and I plan to make you mine. I figured all the getting to know you would come naturally, but if you want to force the issue, we'll set up a schedule. First date, second date, romantic weekends, however you want to play it," he said, then grimaced as Cha-Cha nipped his finger.

Dakota just stared at him. He had just made one of the craziest statements she'd heard in years and he was acting like it was nothing. She had to get the upper hand in this situation and soon. "Look, Nick, the only schedule I'm interested in is the one involving my house. When are you going to get started on it and how long is it going to take?" She didn't care that she sounded snippy and cold, she had to distance herself from the pleasure she knew awaited her in his arms.

"It's already started, baby. Two of my best men went over there today and I thought tomorrow we'd go look at some paint and stains. That okay with you?"

Suddenly Dakota felt ashamed of herself. Nick had been going out of his way to take care of things for her and she was showing him no gratitude whatsoever. She was acting like it was some kind of homage owed to her and nothing could have been further from the truth. He'd housed her, fed her, gotten her car in the shop, rented one for her and was already hard at work on her home. And had she said thank you one time? No, she hadn't.

"Nick, I'm so sorry," she said softly. "You've been doing all these nice things for me and I'm not behaving like I appreciate any of it. I'd love to go look at samples tomorrow, if you can spare the time. And I'll take you out to eat, too. I haven't had a minute to go to the grocery store."

Nick was warmed by her sweet apology, but he was curious about one thing. "Can you cook? 'Cause it sounds to me like I might rate a home-cooked meal one of these days if you know your way around a kitchen."

Dakota raised one eyebrow. "Yes, I can cook. I'm no cordon bleu chef, but I won't poison you. And once I get settled in my new place I will most certainly make a meal for you. If you accept my apology, that is."

Nick dislodged the protesting Cha-Cha and rose, holding out his hand to Dakota. "I can't take anything I haven't earned. You don't owe me anything, baby. Except maybe a walk to the door."

Dakota found herself clinging to Nick's big comforting hand and once again they were facing each other in the foyer. He looked down at her to see what she was going to do, and was immensely pleased when she put her hands on his shoulders and stood on her tiptoes for a kiss.

"See? You like this as much as I do. We have a long time to get to know each other, but there's no reason we can't enjoy this here while we're doing it," he said in a deep, teasing voice.

Her mouth was against his and she murmured, "You talk too much," before giving him a good-night kiss he'd remember for a long time.

The next day was a busy and productive one, due in no small part to Nick. Dakota was able to get all of her personal things moved to her new office thanks to his foresight in making sure that her car was being repaired and she had a rental to drive. Since she didn't have the tedium of a regular deadline to adhere to, she was free to leave the *Herald* for a few hours to go with Nick to look at paint and stain samples. She insisted on meeting him at the home-improvement store but he was equally firm about insisting he pick her up.

"You'll get lost, trust me. This place isn't that easy to find, even for somebody who's been around here for years. I'll come get you and show you how to get there," he said reasonably.

Dakota agreed to let him chauffeur her around, and she was glad she did because the place he took her to was way off the beaten path. It was fascinating, full of unique fixtures and fittings of all types. They spent a long time looking not only at paint and stains, but at cabinetry and wallpaper. By the time they left, Nick knew exactly what Dakota wanted and he'd made some excellent suggestions that she agreed to with no hesitation. She insisted on taking him to lunch and they went to a small seafood restaurant that Nick assured her was one of the best in town. It wasn't fancy, but the appetizing aromas that floated around in the small space made her believe him. After they were seated and the server had taken their orders, she gave him a dazzling smile, one of the first real ones he'd seen on her face.

"What's that smile for?" he asked, giving her one in return.

"I just wish I'd met you before I got involved with that crook Bernard Jackson," she said candidly. "If you'd been in charge of the construction it would have turned out beautifully and I'd be all moved in and happy as a skunk in a pea patch."

Nick burst into laughter. "So what does a big-time city girl like you know about a skunk in a pea patch? Where'd you hear that one?"

"My granny and my daddy say it all the time. For your information, my daddy is from Edgewater, Alabama. He grew up on a teeny little farm, the same farm where I spent most of my summers until we convinced his mother, my Meemaw, to move up to Pittsburgh with us. So I'm not just a big-city girl," she told him. "You don't know anything about me, why don't you just admit it?"

"You're right, Dakota. We don't know much

about each other at all. So why don't you tell me about yourself?" Nick's voice was warm and persuasive, and so were his eyes. Looking at her with unmistakable interest, he suddenly asked, "Did you know there was a singer named Dakota?"

"I certainly do," Dakota replied. "I was named after her. My daddy loves music, jazz and blues in particular, and he named my brother after Johnny Hartman, my sister after Billie Holiday and I was named after Dakota Staton."

"So what did your mama have to say about that? I hope she likes music as much as your daddy does."

"She loves it. She was a singer for a while when she was putting herself through college. She became a nurse, though. And then a college instructor after she got her master's degree. She teaches nursing," Dakota said, then smiled brightly as the server arrived.

He presented her with a big bowl of gumbo and a basket of hot cornbread. Nick had ordered catfish and coleslaw with a side of greens and both meals looked and smelled delicious. She tasted the gumbo and her eyes closed in rapture. "This is the best I've ever had," she said. "And I've eaten plenty in my time. It's incredible. Would you like to taste it?"

She took the spoon from his place setting and dipped it into the bowl and then held it to his lips. He tasted it and agreed it was superb. He returned the favor by letting her taste his catfish, feeding it to her the same way she'd fed him. "Nick you were right, this food is amazing. If I don't watch out, I'm going to weigh a ton from eating out in Chicago," she sighed.

"You need to let that go," Nick said sternly. "I'm not going to tell you too many more times, you're a beautiful woman and you look good. Healthy and sexy, the way a woman's supposed to look."

Dakota was surprised by the quick heat she felt in her cheeks. Luckily, Nick changed the subject. "So are you the baby of the family? The little spoiled princess?"

"I certainly am not spoiled," she protested. "I'm the middle child. Billie is the youngest and she's not spoiled, either. Daddy was good to us, but he wasn't up for any little bratty kids. We had to behave or else. He wasn't afraid to spare the rod, believe me!" She laughed fondly.

"So, tell me about your father. Seems like you like him a lot," Nick said thoughtfully.

"I love him to death. He and my mother are the best parents in the world. Daddy left Alabama after he got out of the service and moved up to Pittsburgh because he could get work in the steel mills. After he worked in the mills for a while he got involved in the union, and he eventually did union work full-time. He's on the executive board now and he still does a lot of negotiating and organizing. He's very well thought of and I'm very proud of him. He's an amazing guy," she said with pride.

Nick looked deep in thought and then stared at her for a minute. "Your daddy wouldn't be Boyd Phillips would he?"

"Yes, he sure is. You've heard of him?"

"I most certainly have. And you're right, he's something else. So that's where you got it from," he mused.

"Got what?" Dakota asked with a puzzled look on her face.

"All that backbone," Nick replied. "I was wondering where a little princess like you got all that spunk from and now I know. You got it from your daddy," he said with a grin that angered Dakota for some reason.

"How dare you call me that? You don't know

me at all and you have the nerve to call me a princess? Do you get any exercise other than jumping to conclusions?" she asked hotly.

Nick just laughed, which made her even angrier. "See how you're reacting? I pay you a compliment and you get all bent out of shape. That's what I mean, darlin'. You're all regal and refined, but you got this edge to you that makes you tough and smart. That's a good combination, baby. You got heat in your blood; it makes you a real woman, that's all I'm saying."

Dakota wished with all her heart that she had a double martini in front of her instead of the glass of sweet tea. Nick was rattling her badly and she didn't like it. To be perfectly honest, she liked the way he talked to her because he was down-to-earth and confident and said whatever was on his mind and that was a rarity among the men she knew. But there was something about the tone of his voice and the damnably sexy twinkle in his eyes that affected her deeply and that's what she really didn't like. She couldn't afford to get caught up with a man like Nick. Nothing but trouble could come of it and she'd already experienced enough man trouble to last her the rest of her life.

She was trying to think of the right words to put Nick in check once and for all when he said something that made whatever she was going to say vanish like a puff of smoke.

"By the way, I found Bernard. You'll have your investment returned within forty-eight hours, and I don't think he'll be trying his old tricks on anybody else."

Dakota had never quite understood the meaning of the word *speechless* until then. She couldn't have said a word if her hope of salvation depended on it.

Two weeks had gone by since Nick's amazing announcement and Dakota was still stunned by its impact. She was grateful that a big story had come across her desk and she had something to keep her mind occupied, but she was still rocked by the casual way Nick had told her that he'd kept his word and run Bernard Jackson down like the sniveling weasel he was. She couldn't get Nick out of her mind and the thoughts she was having about him were most inappropriate. Nick Hunter was keeping her awake at night and she didn't know what to do about it. But for the moment she could direct her wayward imagination and concentrate on work.

Zane was seated in her cubicle, chatting about the investigative article on which she was working, and she was actually able to keep her mind off Nick for a while, something which was a great relief to her. She had grown to like and admire Zane more and more as she got to know him. He was warm and friendly with a dry, self-deprecating humor that she found adorable. And he was also brilliant. She was totally engrossed in their conversation when Toni Brandon popped her head over Dakota's cubicle and gave the two of them a long stare.

"Boss, I think it's time you let this lady out of her coop for lunch. You two have been at it for two hours and she deserves a break," Toni said firmly. "And so do you. Would you like to come to lunch with us?"

"Uhh, I'd love to but I have a conference call in—" he glanced at his watch. "Wow, it's right now as a matter of fact. Give me a rain check, will ya?"

Only Dakota noticed the slight reddening of the tops of his ears. Toni was utterly oblivious, but Dakota was sure that Zane was attracted to her new friend. Very attracted, as a matter of fact. But since Toni was engaged, there was nothing to be done. She sighed deeply as she neatly stacked the papers on her desk and opened her bottom drawer for her shoulder bag. Toni misinterpreted the reason for her sigh and raised an eager eyebrow.

"Umm-hmm. There's something on your mind and you need someone closemouthed to confide in," she said with a serious look on her face. She smiled brightly, the corners of her beautiful eyes crinkling. "Luckily for you, I happen to be the perfect person. I say we blow this pop stand and go out for some serious girl talk."

Dakota sighed. She and Toni had gone to lunch a few times and were well on the way to becoming good friends. It sounded like just the thing to her, but she had to beg off. "My sister is coming into town. My brother has her convinced that I'm living out of the back of my car and she won't rest until she sees with her own eyes that I'm not homeless," she said apologetically. "She knows I'm staying at Nick's but she insists on coming. I'm glad, though. My sister is my best friend."

"Well, that's sounds like a party! You got any wine?"

Dakota nodded her head and was about to say something when Toni held up one hand. "Forget trying to say no, I don't understand the meaning of that word. Ask my parents, they'll tell you I was never an obedient child. Just give me your address and I'll meet you there in an hour with everything else. We'll have a ball."

Sure enough, Toni got to the apartment before Billie arrived and she carried with her two shopping bags that were filled with "everything else." There was a cheese tray, an array of fresh vegetables with a yummy-looking dip and a fruit salad filled with chunks of ripe watermelon, blackberries, blueberries, pineapple and cantaloupe. The second bag held a crusty loaf of French bread, stone wheat crackers and smoked turkey. Dakota was touched that Toni had gone to so much trouble for her, but Toni blew off her thanks. They had arranged all the food on the hideous dining-room table while Cha-Cha made frantic noises of extreme hunger. Toni picked her up and tickled her under the chin.

"Consider this a welcome to the big city. I'm going to be trying to get all in your business, so I owe it to you to feed you well," she said with a sly wink. "When is your sister getting in? Didn't you have to pick her up at the airport or something?"

"Billie? Honey, she knows Chicago like the back of her hand. And knowing Billie, some Chicago Bull or Bear or White Sox or Cub picked her up in his Hummer or sent a car for her. Or one of the other random millionaires who worship at her feet," Dakota said fondly. "Wait until she gets here, you'll understand what I mean."

With perfect timing the bell rang and Dakota's eyes glowed. "What timing! C'mon and meet my little sister. She's who I want to be when I grow up," she laughed.

She ran to the foyer and flung the door open. There stood a thinner, taller version of Dakota with a uniformed chauffeur bearing her luggage and a shopping bag from a boutique in Milan. "Hey, big sister! You're looking fabulous," Billie said as she threw her arms around Dakota.

They hugged long and hard and when they finally let go, Dakota shook her head. "*You* look fabulous, as always. I still can't believe we swam in the same gene pool," she said with affection.

Toni was trying not to stare, but she gave up the pretense. "You didn't tell me your sister is *Wilhelmina!*"

Wilhelmina was the name Billie used professionally. She was indeed a model, and a very successful one. Her picture regularly graced *Vogue, Elle, Essence* and *Cosmopolitan*. And she had a magnificent contract with a major cosmetics firm as well as being sought after for all the runway shows. Toni was staring at her with admiration. "We just finished an article on the world of modeling and your name was mentioned several times. It's just as well I didn't know you were related or I'd have begged Dakota mercilessly for an interview with you. I didn't notice the resemblance before, but you two look just alike!"

"Except for the height and the hips," Dakota mumbled. "Come on in here, girl, so this poor man can put down your stuff."

Not surprisingly, the chauffeur didn't seem to be the least bit put out; on the contrary he was behaving as though it were his personal pleasure to tote and carry for the lovely Billie. Dakota recognized the glazed look in his eyes for what it was. Her beautiful younger sister had racked up yet another conquest. While the bags were put into the bedroom and the smitten driver was sent on his way after refusing the generous tip he was offered, Dakota looked Billie over. She was simply gorgeous; there was no other way to describe her. They shared the same caramel skin and the same abundant black hair, and their features were very similar, as Toni had noticed. But Billie was six feet tall and as slender as a reed. Hers was the body Dakota had always longed for. Even though she adored her baby sister with all her heart, she couldn't stop a twinge of jealousy when she looked at Billie's long, thin arms, her sculpted collarbones, her chic lack of bosom and her lean, boyish hips. What a contrast to Dakota's big butt, rounded hips and lush breasts.

Toni and Billie hit it off at once and were chattering away like two old friends. It turned out that they knew some of the same people due to Toni's connections in the world of fashion and beauty. And Toni had once modeled herself, which was really not a surprise, given her striking good looks.

"I just couldn't stay as thin as they wanted me to," Toni said frankly. "When I was young the weight stayed off, but the older I got, the harder it got. When I looked at myself in the mirror one night after I had just made myself throw up, I said to hell with it. So I left the business. I did some plus-sized modeling for a while, but I used the money I'd saved to get my degree and I got out with my self-esteem intact. Modeling is a rough world for a young girl."

They were sitting in the dining room sipping wine and picking over the remains of their feast. Billie was uncharacteristically quiet during Toni's remarks. She tossed back the rest of her drink and looked around the room. "This place isn't as bad as you said it was, Dakota. It's a little over the top, but he really has a good eye. In New York or Paris this place would be the bomb, girl."

Toni agreed. "It's fresh, daring and in-your-face. Much like the man who decorated it, I assume?"

Dakota groaned and dropped her head. Toni and Billie started talking about her as though she weren't there, which ordinarily would have driven her mad. But today she just lacked the strength to deal with it and let them go at it.

"So have you met this man? He must be something because my big sister is not being herself, to put it mildly," Billie said.

"Yes, I met him and he's a big ol' hunk of man.

Very tall, with Smokey Robinson green eyes and a voice like Barry White. If I wasn't engaged, I might try to snag him myself," Toni said candidly.

Billie had to examine Toni's big sparkly diamond engagement ring and while she was doing that, Dakota's cell phone buzzed and she picked it up impatiently. "Hello?"

She tried to hide her pleased expression but failed. "I'd love to, but I have company. My friend Toni is here and so is my sister…. Well, yes, but Billie just got here and I'm sure she doesn't feel like going out," she demurred.

"Yes, I do," Billie said loudly. "When have I ever not wanted to go somewhere, especially if there's food involved. Where we goin'?"

Dakota gave her sister a calculating stare. She spoke into the phone again with more assurance. "Okay, fine. Where shall we meet you?"

In a minute or so she'd disconnected the phone and sat back with a smug look. "That was Nick. He's coming to take us all out to dinner," she announced in the same voice she would have used to say that a dead mouse was in the kitchen.

Toni and Billie lit up. "Well don't just sit there, girl, you've got to get dressed!" Billie told her.

Dakota looked down at her slacks and her silk blouse. "What's wrong with what I have on?"

Toni and Billie looked and each other and said in unison, "Everything!"

Chapter 6

Dakota allowed Toni and Billie to bully her into the shower while they laid out what they determined was more appropriate garb for a date. She took her time in the hot steamy water, trying to get her bearings. She had a plan, a dangerous one to be sure, but it was a plan nonetheless. She and Nick had spent quite a bit of time together in the past couple of weeks, and she was, despite her normal steely resolve, becoming quite interested in Nick. He was funny and engaging and told great stories. He had good manners and he also had good sense.

And he actually did what he said he was going to do, she thought as she lathered her body in fragrant bubbles from the bath gel Billie had thrust in her hand. Most importantly, he seemed to genuinely like her. And he also seemed to be really attracted to her, every inch of her. That was the basis for her plan, which was actually more of a test.

She rubbed the scented gel over her breasts while she thought about what she was about to do. She was going to toss Billie at Nick and see what happened. No man was able to resist her little sister and she had no doubt that Nick would prove to be one of those men who melted like butter in a hot skillet when they got a look at her endless legs, dreamy eyes and slender, sexy body. The thought of him drooling all over Billie was daunting, and a pain pierced her heart as she realized how disappointed she'd be when she saw that dumbfounded look on his face. Her hands paused for a moment and she suddenly had to wipe her eyes, which were burning for some reason. The burning doubled when she got soap in her eyes and she had to let the water from the shower wash away the irritating suds. This was something she had to do, dammit. She was already having hot dreams about him every night; there was no point in letting her guard down any further unless she knew he was really sincere about her. *I have to do this. I have to know,* she thought fiercely.

In the meantime, Billie was showing Toni the present she'd brought for Dakota. "I saw this in Milan and I could just see her in it," Billie said. "Isn't it perfect?"

It was a simple silk-and-cotton-blend dress that had a scoop neck and a deep back with criss-crossed straps. It fit close to the body through the bodice, and flared out into a full skirt that would end above the knee. It was sleeveless with deeply-cut armholes and it would show off Dakota's arms and her stupendous breasts perfectly. Toni agreed at once.

"It's beautiful, and that indigo color will look great with her skin tone. Now all she needs are some shoes to go with it," Toni said.

Billie triumphantly pulled out a pair of Ferragamo sandals with a higher heel than Toni had ever seen her friend wear. "These match it perfectly and she's going to wear them or go barefoot," Billie said firmly. "I'm sure she hasn't told you this, but her self-esteem took a beating last year thanks to

KIMANI PRESS™

An Important Message from the Publisher

Dear Reader,

Because you've chosen to read one of our fine novels, I'd like to say "thank you"! And, as a special way to say thank you, I'm offering to send you two Kimani Romance™ novels and two surprise gifts – absolutely FREE! These books will keep it real with true-to-life African-American characters that turn up the heat and sizzle with passion.

Please enjoy the free books and gifts with our compliments...

Linda Gill

Publisher, Kimani Press

Peel off Seal and Place Inside...

THE EDITORS' THANK YOU
FROM KIMANI PRESS

Two NEW Kimani Romance™ Novels
Two exciting surprise gifts

I have placed my
Editor's "Thank You" Free Gifts
seal in the space provided at
right. Please send me 2 FREE
books, and my 2 FREE Mystery
Gifts. I understand that I am
under no obligation to purchase
anything further, as explained on
the back of this card.

**PLACE
FREE GIFTS
SEAL
HERE**

168 XDL ELWZ   368 XDL ELXZ

FIRST NAME	LAST NAME

ADDRESS

APT.#	CITY

STATE/PROV.	ZIP/POSTAL CODE

Thank You!

BUSINESS REPLY MAIL
FIRST-CLASS MAIL   PERMIT NO. 717-003   BUFFALO, NY

POSTAGE WILL BE PAID BY ADDRESSEE

THE READER SERVICE
3010 WALDEN AVE
PO BOX 1867
BUFFALO NY 14240-9952

NO POSTAGE
NECESSARY
IF MAILED
IN THE
UNITED STATES

this doofus she was dating. I hated him," she said, her eyes glinting at his memory. "He wasn't man enough for her, anybody could see that, but for some reason she thought he was the stuff, you know? His name was Jonah, of all things, and he was this mealy-mouthed corporate tool, a lobbyist or something. D.C. is full of bottom-feeders.

"Anyway, I always thought he was with Dakota because of who she is. You know what I mean, her name, her fame, and her brains. He was riding on her coattails, as far I was concerned. He was a control freak, too. He had emotional abuse written all over him. He used to try to get her to lose weight, used to watch every mouthful she took and made little cracks about her needing to join a gym."

Toni made a face. "Been there, done that. I know the kind. The 'you-have-such-a-pretty-face' kind. They swear up and down they love you just for you, but every other minute they're trying to get you to go on a diet. I dated this one schmuck who told me we couldn't have sex again until I lost five pounds."

"Ooohh, no he didn't! What did you tell him?"

"That the sex wasn't good enough for me to

miss a meal and for him to lose my number. That's one of the reasons I love my man so much. He's from Albania and they love meat on the bones," she giggled.

"Yeah, well, as much as that creep Jonah loved being on Dakota's arm because she knew everybody in Washington, he had the nerve to try and change her. This was after he'd proposed, mind you. Told her he didn't want people calling them Jonah and the whale, can you imagine? And then, just when Dakota was actually considering getting liposuction, he up and leaves her for this emaciated heifer with the IQ of a turnip." Billie's face turned deep red with anger as she recalled how devastated her sister had been.

"She was better off without him, of course and she knows that. But it was still a blow to the heart she didn't deserve. That's part of the reason she's so skittish about getting involved with a man. She doesn't trust them at all," Billie confided. "And that's too bad because this Nick sounds like—"

"Sounds like what?" Dakota had come out of the shower just in time to hear the end of Billie's speech.

"Sounds like a man who's going to be on time. You need to get stepping unless you plan to go out in that towel. Here's your dress, but where is your underwear?"

Dakota stared at the beautiful dress in dismay. It was lovely, just right for a summer-night date. But she couldn't wear something like that! "Billie it's beautiful, but I don't think…"

"I don't think you have time to argue," Toni said pertly. "Put on your undies and sit down so we can put on your makeup and do your hair. I've been meaning to talk to you about your attire anyway. You and I need to do some power shopping. You don't dress to show off your figure at all," she fussed.

Dakota did as she was bid and put on a pair of thong panties and the only strapless bra she owned. Luckily, it was like new since she'd only worn it twice. She slipped into a summer kimono and obediently took a seat on the bed where both Toni and Billie attacked her with highly-skilled gusto. When they were finished, she didn't recognize herself. Her skin glowed with its light application of foundation, a touch of blush and a soft juicy gloss the color of ripe cherries. Her eyes were huge and smoky with the application of dark charcoal shadow, indigo eyeliner that was smudged for a subtle seduction, and a ton of very expensive mascara. A bit of gold highlighter under her brows and on her cheekbones and she was finished. Her hair was a tousled mass of curls held up by some sparkly hair ornaments Billie had gotten at a flea market in Paris. When she put on the dress, which fit perfectly, Dakota didn't recognize herself. "Is that me? That's not me," she murmured as she admired her reflection.

Nick ignored the doorbell and gave his customary loud knock. Billie held up her hand. "A lady never opens the door for a date if she can help it. Toni, you get the door while I find some earrings," she instructed. Toni went to answer the door with Cha-Cha hot on her heels. The cat had ESP where her man was concerned and she knew his knock.

Toni let Nick in and greeted him. "Dakota will be right out. Would you like something to drink?" she asked sweetly. Before he could answer, Dakota entered the room and Nick's ability to speak seemed to desert him. He literally devoured her with his eyes, looking her up and down as though he couldn't get enough of the vision of loveliness that had come into his view.

When he regained speech, it was unlike his

usual playful banter. With utter seriousness he said, "Damn. So this is what you've been hiding from me all this time, huh? You look beautiful, baby. You need to wear more dresses. You're made for a pretty dress and that dress is made for you. I almost don't want to take you out, you look so good," he said reverently.

"Oh, but you have to," a new voice said. "I believe I was promised a meal and I'm hungry," Billie announced.

She stood there with her arms akimbo and her long legs shown off to their full extent by a micromini skirt made of black faille and a leopard-print halter top. She was wearing Christian Louboutin platform shoes and her hair was wild and loose. Dakota was aware that her body refused to take a breath as she waited for Nick's reaction to her sister. It was a while in coming, but he walked over and kissed Dakota on the cheekbone. "You smell good, baby. You look good, you smell good and I already know you taste good. I don't have an appetite for anything but you," he said in a low, compelling voice. She stared into his eyes and saw nothing there but the green fire that heralded another one of his sizzling kisses and she suddenly felt the same way. She was about to melt into his arms when Billie interrupted the moment.

Jangling her heavy gold bracelets, she laughed at the two of them. "Y'all are pitiful. Feed me good and you're on your own for dessert. I have a feeling I know what it's going to be," she said cheekily. "You must be Nick. I'm Billie and I'm *hungry.* Can we get some barbecue?"

Toni, in the meantime, was waving goodbye. "My work here is done. I have to meet Ivan so I'm taking my leave of you good folks. Billie, take notes," she said merrily as she closed the door behind her.

Nick finally seemed to realize there was someone else in the room and shook the hand Billie offered him. "All right ladies, let's go. I know a place that serves the best barbecue in Chicago, you'll love it." He took Dakota's hand and glanced at Billie's lithe form. "They have real big portions, too."

Billie looked around the restaurant Nick had chosen with avid interest. "Oh yeah, these folks can throw down with some barbecue," she said as she sniffed the air with anticipation. It was a plain-looking place, nothing fancy. The floor was well-worn black-and-white linoleum and there were big booths around the edge of the room, with tables in the middle. All the tables had white paper tablecloths and there was a roll of paper towels on each table in lieu of napkins. It certainly wasn't trendy, but it was immaculately clean and there was some great music playing and everyone seemed to be enjoying their meals, even though the aromatic sauce involved the use of big bibs by the patrons to avoid the inevitable sauce stains. Billie rubbed her hands together gleefully. "I want some of everything and a big ol' slab of ribs. If they have lemonade, I want some of that, too, with extra ice. I'm going to wash my hands, I'll be right back," she said as she slid out of the red vinyl booth.

Nick stood quickly as she left and watched her as she walked across the room drawing a lot of male attention. He sat down even closer to Dakota with a worried look on his face. "She's not going to stuff her face and then…" he made a gesture that indicated making herself sick. Dakota laughed at his concern.

"Honey, she's not bulimic! And she's obviously

not anorexic, either. My sister eats like a horse, always has. She's just got the good genes in the family and never gains weight. Not an ounce," she said, smoothing her dress over her thighs.

Nick turned all his attention to the woman at his side. "You look real good, baby. You always look pretty, but tonight you look the way you should. You should always wear something that shows off your legs. You have some beautiful legs, girl, why do you keep them covered up?"

Billie returned to the table in time to hear that remark. "That's a good question, babycakes. Why do you always wear pants? If I had legs like yours people would get tired of looking at them 'cause I'd have 'em on display every day."

To Dakota's horror, Billie turned to Nick and began to regale him with tales of their youth. "When we were growing up, I was so jealous of my big sister I couldn't stand it! She was the smartest girl in school and not just our school, the whole city! She was known all over the state for her SAT scores and her awards," Billie reported. "She was everything, you hear me? She was a cheerleader, she was Homecoming Queen, Prom Queen, Most Beautiful Teen, you name it, and she was it. And the boys, well, just forget it. When I was in high school I never brought a boy home, ever."

Nick went along with it, smiling as Billie told her story. "And why was that?"

"Because they took one look at her and fell in love, that's why! She had all that pretty hair, that perfect skin and that Beyoncé body, and I was tall and skinny. I had no chance whatsoever," Billie laughed. "Dakota was smart and popular and stacked, and I was taller than all the boys in my class. And skinny as a rail. My nickname in high school was Beanie, short for Stringbean."

By now the food had come and Dakota was relieved to see the platters. Maybe now Billie would shut up. She tried to end the conversation by saying, "Obviously she's exaggerating. Eat before it gets cold, Billie."

After holding hands with Nick and Dakota and saying grace, Billie dug in with good appetite, but she kept on talking. "All my teachers wanted to know why I wasn't as smart as Dakota and all the boys wanted to know why I didn't have boobies like Dakota. She was a hard act to follow, let me tell you!"

Dakota wanted to dive under the table, especially when she saw how much Nick was enjoying this. She had to resort to imitating the squinty look her mother always employed to get them to behave when they were in public, and Billie finally took the hint. But she wasn't through talking, not by a long shot. She simply turned her attention to Nick. "So tell me about yourself. Who are you and where do you come from? I think I hear a southern accent there." She beamed at him as she licked a little sauce off her pinkie.

"I'm from Georgia, originally. Grew up dirt-poor, me and my brother Paul. We got tired of picking peaches, pecans, cotton and whatever else they were paying people to pick and we went into the army. Came out in one piece and moved to Chicago and went into construction. End of story."

Billie arched her eyebrow while she reached for another piece of cornbread from the heaping basket in the middle of the table. "I have a feeling you left a few things out. Did you always want to build things? Dakota says you're like a genius with building and remodeling and land development. She says you're a true success story and that you're a real man," she said in a voice devoid of guile.

Nick looked over at Dakota who was wishing with all her heart that she was an only child. "Is that what Miss Lady says about me? I think she exaggerated a little. I'm just a plain working man, trying to get some bills paid, that's all."

Dakota rolled her eyes at him and gave his hard, muscular bicep a swat. "Oh stop it. I hate false modesty," she said with a frown.

"Billie, he really is a genius. Did you notice how gorgeous the apartment building is? He did all that himself. He gutted the whole building and restored it just the way it was when it was built. You should see some of the things his company has done. Houses, apartments, commercial buildings, you can't imagine what he can do. He has more than talent, he has skill and vision and an amazing work ethic. He's—" She stopped talking because Nick's mouth came down on hers.

When the brief kiss was over he turned to Billie with a grin. "It's the only way I can get her to shut up," he said smugly.

"I've had it with both of you. I'm going to the ladies' room and I may or may not come back," Dakota said and rose to leave. Nick stood and watched her walk quickly across the room. Even more men were watching her than had watched Billie and he thought that maybe she had the right idea about wearing pants in public. He was looking a little grumpy when he sat down.

Billie was staring at him intently and it was obvious that she had something on her mind so he invited her to unburden herself. "Go ahead. Get it out of your system."

"Well, I can see that threats won't work with you, although I did learn to gut fish pretty efficiently when my daddy took us fishing. But that's a story for another day. My sister is a very special woman, Nick, and if you can't treat her the way she deserves to be treated, you need to walk away now because I won't have her hurt. The last man she was involved with treated her really badly and it's not going to happen again. If you want to play, you need to find another playmate, that's all I'm saying," she said. All traces of the friendly, sweet Billie were gone; she was utterly serious.

Nick actually smiled when she got through. "I'm glad you love your sister. You also like her and that's real nice. Family is all we have in this world when it comes down to it. You don't have to worry about me mistreating your sister in any way. In case you haven't noticed, I think she's pretty special, too. As a matter of fact, I intend to—"

"You intend to what?" Dakota said as she took her seat again.

Nick turned his brilliant eyes on her and drank in her radiant beauty. "I intend to show you the work on your house," he hedged. Turning back to Billie, he asked, "You want to come along?"

Dakota was stunned when she saw the changes that had been wrought in her brownstone. The floors were perfect, with the honey-oak stain she and Nick had picked out. All the woodwork gleamed and there was a subtle satin finish that glowed under the light. The lighting fixtures were in place, all of them the Mission-style reproduction pieces she'd originally requested. The kitchen cabinets were in place, not the shoddy ones Bernard had stuck her with, but beautifully balanced and properly hung glass-fronted cupboards that she couldn't wait to see filled with her belongings. The slate countertops and the matching backsplash behind the sink were just what she'd imagined. Billie ran all over the house inspecting while Dakota leaned against the counters and tried to collect herself.

She covered her mouth with her hand and tears gathered in her eyes as she looked around at all the work that had been done in such a short period of time.

"What's the matter, baby? Don't you like it?" Nick sounded alarmed.

Dakota went to him at once and wrapped her arms around his waist, resting her head on his chest. She looked up at him with eyes made starry by the tears. "Nick, don't be ridiculous. It's wonderful! It looks even better than I imagined it from the beginning. You and your crew did an amazing job on this, just beautiful. Thank you so much for this," she whispered. She stood on her tiptoes to kiss him, something he helped her with by leaning down to her waiting lips.

It was a long, deliberate kiss that fused them closer together than ever. Nick took his time with her, teasing her juicy lips, sucking and tantalizing them with his lips and tongue until he couldn't take any more teasing and the sensual plunder began for real. She was faintly aware that he'd picked her up and that her bottom was now on the work island in the center of the room, but it was an abstract notion. All she knew was how he was making her feel, the waves of raw passion that rocked her to her core, the urge to feel more of him, to touch him and be touched by him in the most intimate way possible. She didn't want to stop, she wanted more and more of the delicious sensations he was creating and he knew it. He knew what she wanted as she moved her hands over his big shoulders and he wanted it, too, more than anything.

"I want to take you home, baby," he said in a husky whisper. "I want to give you the kind of loving you need, Dakota. You need me as much as I need you and I don't want to wait any more. I want you, baby."

"Let's go, Nick. Let's go right now," she said breathlessly.

And if Billie hadn't run down the stairs in her platform shoes they might have slipped out the door and left the poor thing standing there in an empty house. Nick gave a harsh laugh that was anything but amused, and Dakota just looked stricken when she realized that their magic moment was over for now. They pulled away from each other with great reluctance, and Nick lifted her off the counter and set her on the floor. He gave her one last squeeze and a kiss on her earlobe. "Your day is coming, Miss Lady. It's coming real soon, baby."

Billie, bless her, tried to act as though nothing was amiss and asked Nick how he'd managed to recoup Dakota's investment. "All she told me was that you'd found the scoundrel and she was going to get her money back, but I didn't get any details." She walked all the way into the kitchen and ran her hands over the exquisite countertop. "This is so nice, I can't get over it," she murmured. She leaned against the counter and repeated her question. "How did you do it?"

Nick pulled Dakota in front of him and locked his arms around her waist. "There isn't much to tell. I have a friend who has a friend who knows some people. They located him in his hideout in the islands and they went and got him for me. I'd a gone myself but I had some things to attend to. They brought him here to the house and we took a little tour. I told him the lady who owned it was a personal friend of mine and I didn't appreciate the way he handled his business, so, if he didn't mind, I'd appreciate getting her money back. And I also suggested he not try to work in the state of Illinois again because it didn't seem like his heart was in his work. That's all."

Dakota and Billie stared at each other, their eyes huge. It was obvious from Nick's studiedly casual delivery that a lot more had gone on, but he wasn't telling what had actually happened. It didn't stop Billie from asking, though.

"Did you hit him?" she asked eagerly.

He nodded over Dakota's head so she couldn't see him. "Of course not, what kind of man do you think I am?"

While Dakota turned to smile up at him, Billie held up her fingers like a gun, mouthing the words "Did you shoot him?"

As though he hadn't seen her little pantomime, Nick said smoothly, "When you're dealing with a punk you don't have to shoot, and most times you don't even have to show them a gun. You just make them an offer they can't refuse."

When Dakota laughed in appreciation of the quote from *The Godfather,* Billie pumped her fist over her head. Nick had just confirmed what she suspected, that he'd done much more than have a quiet little chat with Bernard Jackson. *Hot damn! Now* that's *a man,* she thought.

Nick continued to hold Dakota until she turned around to face him. Looking up at him earnestly, she said, "I still think you should take more for the house, Nick. Paying for the materials and the labor doesn't amount to the same thing. I feel as though I'm taking advantage of you. You need to let me pay you the market value for this property."

He looked deeply into her luminous eyes and it was difficult for him to keep his lips from hers. "Look, baby. When your neighbors saw that Hunter Construction sign in your yard, they knew something was up. I've already gotten seven jobs as a result of doing your house, so don't even worry about the money. This is like an investment for me that's already paid me back seven times over."

"But Nick," she murmured, only to have him kiss her quiet.

Billie watched them affectionately and then made a great show of yawning widely. "Wow, I had no idea it was so late! International flying really takes it out of me. I need to get to bed," she said pointedly.

Nick drove them back to the apartment building and walked them to the door, which he unlocked and insisted on entering first. "That's just my way," he explained to Billie. "Just in case somebody who's not supposed to be here decides to act crazy," he said gruffly. And sure enough, Cha-Cha came barreling out and leaped into Nick's arms.

Billie broke up the love fest that was about to begin by taking the cat with her. "C'mon with me, you little trollop," she said playfully. "You can help me unpack, I'm sure I've got some expensive things for you to sink your claws into."

The two of them went off to the bedroom, leaving Nick and Dakota alone. She took his hand to lead him into the living room. "Come sit down with me," she invited. "Would you like something to drink?"

Nick sat down on the big leather sofa and pulled her into his lap. "What I want right now, I can't get because your little sister is in the next room."

Dakota ran her fingers through the hair at his temples and gave him a seductive smile. "What would you do if we were alone?" She deliberately arched her back so that her breasts were cushioned against his chest.

Nick's expression became fiercely intense and his hands tightened around her waist. "Don't play with me, woman. If I had you alone right now I'd have those clothes off you and you'd be naked in my bed. I'd be deep inside you and you'd be calling my name and clawing my back up," he said in a deep growl.

Dakota's breath caught in her throat. "Nick, you make me sound like a cat in heat!"

His big hand slid under her dress and caressed her smooth thigh and she gasped in surprise. The warmth of his skin and the feel of his calloused palm made her tremble. He smiled at her reaction and flexed his strong fingers over her soft skin. "You're not *in* heat, you *are* heat, baby. You're gonna set me on fire, Miss Lady." He kissed her lips, her neck and her collarbones, breathing her name softly. Suddenly he set her abruptly off his lap and stood. "Look here, woman, you're not gonna drive me crazy up in here. Come walk me to the door and we'll continue this when your company is gone."

Dakota's mouth fell open from surprise and it was immediately filled with Nick's kiss, long and tender and sensual. She was trying to decide how she felt about what he'd just said when he said something even more surprising. He put his hands on her shoulders and stroked her arms while looking at her as though it was the first time he'd ever seen anyone so lovely. "I'll bet you look even better with nothing on. I can't wait to see that beautiful body naked," he whispered before kissing her again.

Now Dakota knew exactly what she was feeling; it was pure panic and nothing else.

Chapter 7

Dakota spent most of the next morning out in the field, but when she returned to the office, Toni was waiting to pounce on her. "There you are! I was about to call Missing Persons and report you gone. You can't leave a nosey woman like me dangling, I have to know things. How'd it go last night?"

She sat on the chair next to Dakota's desk and waited for her response. "And don't think you can lie to me, I already got the scoop from Billie," she warned.

"See? Y'all are ganging up on me," Dakota said. "Well if Billie already told you everything, you don't need to hear it from me." When Toni looked as though she was going to explode, Dakota relented.

"It was a lot of fun. He's as nice as he is good-looking and he's very sexy. Very. And wait until you see what he's done to my place! He says I can take occupancy next week. He told us how he found the guy who'd conned me and how he got my money back, but I don't believe he told us the whole story. He gave us the PG version, there's an R-rated version of the truth out there. I have the distinct impression that Nick gave Mr. Jackson more than a stern talking-to, if you get my drift."

Toni nodded, even as she asked another question. "Does that bother you, the thought that he might be capable of getting physical when the situation calls for it?"

Dakota thought about Nick, his kindness, his strength, his work ethic and his personality. And she thought about the people Jackson had conned in the past and the fact that they didn't have a Nick to step in for them. She gave a Toni a secretive little smile and said no. "It's not like he's a thug-for-hire, he just does what he has to do to get the results he wants. He's a very gentle person on the inside, but he's not going to put up with much," she said dreamily.

"So it sounds like you two are a match made in heaven. He's obviously crazy about you. He can't keep his eyes off you and I'll bet he can't keep his hands off you, either. So what's the next stop on the Love Train?" Toni said with a throaty laugh.

Instead of returning the laughter, Dakota looked glum. "He wants to see me naked, Toni. *I* don't want to see me naked! There must be some way I can forestall the inevitable until I lose some weight," she muttered.

Toni frowned. "You really need to quit, girl. You won't find any sympathy here. I had a terrible self-esteem issue when I was modeling. I was driven to bulimia before I got a grip. Everybody is not meant to be the same size. And every man isn't interested in someone who's built like your sister. Nick obviously likes what he sees and what he feels when he puts his arms around you. You have a good figure. You're what they call 'cute in the face and small in the waist' and you need to stop trippin' before you turn Nick off. Men want a woman who's confident in herself in the bedroom and out," she reminded Dakota. "And as smart and accomplished and brilliant as you are you haven't figured that out yet?"

Now Dakota was laughing because no one except her mother and her sister had ever talked to her like this. "No! I mean yes, of course I know it. I get it, I get the whole thing about loving yourself and feeling confident and all that. I know it all, I know all the mantras, all the buzzwords, and I know that I'm being ridiculous. And I guess I don't look that bad," she mused. "I don't have cellulite," she added brightly.

Toni shook her head as she watched Dakota mercilessly twisting a paper clip into pieces. "Not good enough. You've got to be able to look at yourself butt-naked in the mirror and love what you see. Not tolerate it or put up with it until you look like someone whose body structure has nothing to do with yours. You've got to *love* your body. That's going to make your man love it even more than he does. And I know just what you need to do," she said firmly. "You're going to be in a fashion show. And once you stroll down that runway, you're going to think about yourself in a totally different way, I guarantee it."

"I'm gonna do *what?*"

"Leave it all to me, chick, when I get through with you you'll be a new woman," Toni said with a wink.

"Toni, I'm not going to be in any fashion show, are you nuts?"

"This one is different. It's for ladies only and it's for charity. And all the models are size fourteen and up. This is for real women with exquisite clothes modeled by real women. And you, my conflicted little friend, are going to do this and do it well. Once you've strutted your stuff out there you're going to feel like a new person. Trust me!"

And suddenly, as improbable as it seemed, Dakota did.

A loud crash in the main part of the office made both Dakota and Toni leap to their feet and then burst into laughter. Billie was strolling across the office and a minor collision had ensued when two reporters had caught sight of her in all her glory. She was wearing well-worn jeans with a couple of artistic rips here and there and a tight white tailored shirt that was tied under her midriff. Her hair was pulled back with a wide headband and with her Chanel sunglasses perched on her forehead and a huge pair of silver hoop earrings, she looked like every man's fantasy come to life. She was looking for Dakota and was totally unaware of the chaos she was leaving behind her.

She smiled when she saw her sister waving at her. "There you are! I'm hungry, can we go eat now?"

Billie, of course, thought the fashion show was a fabulous idea and got right on board with it. "You owe me anyway. You think I don't know that you planned to toss me at Nick to see what he would do? This is your payback for trying to use me as a sacrificial lamb," she said haughtily.

"And don't say you didn't do it because I used to do the same thing to you when I was in college. I'd bring some boy to the house and if he started drooling over you I'd dump him. You know I used to do that, so don't try and play me."

"Aw, baby sis, I wasn't thinking of you as a lamb. More like a *goat,*" Dakota laughed. "I admit it, that twisted idea did cross my mind. I was wrong, I was wrong, I was wrong. Isn't there any way I can prove how sorry I am?" she asked winsomely.

"Why, yes there is. You can let me take you shopping and then let me show you how to work a runway. Then you can take care of your business with that big gorgeous hunk of Nick. I'll consider the matter settled then," she said mischievously.

They were having lunch at a little bistro near the office and Toni raised her glass of water in agreement. "Hear, hear! You need to get some clothes that fit your body and show it off. You're what, a size sixteen? The way you dress makes you look like a twenty sometimes," she said frankly. "No more pantsuits for you, girl, you need to work the words *skirt* and *dress* into your fashion vocabulary."

Dakota took another bite of her grilled chicken salad before answering. "Yeah, but a lot of times I'm in situations where I need to be wearing pants. It's cold in the morgue," she protested. "And if I'm at the scene of a really gross murder, I can't be wearing my good shoes. Do you know what slogging through a muddy field would do to those little Ferragamos you bought me?"

"Okay, *ewww,*" Billie said. "But you can keep some workmanlike jeans or khakis in the car and at the office and still manage to look hot when you aren't covering the crime of the century," she said with a shudder.

"Trust us," Toni said persuasively. "We're not going to turn you into a hoochie. We're just going to show you how to show off those curves. You'll like it and Nick will love it. Look, I've got an interview in about fifteen minutes, so I've got to dash. But tonight, we *shop*," she said, raising her glass of mineral water.

The two sisters finished their meals while Billie continued to extol Nick's virtues. "I just want to know how you've managed to keep your hands off him," she said as she speared the fruit garnish off Dakota's plate. "That's a whole lotta man you got there, sis. He's just what you need. Somebody who's confident and strong and capable, just like he is. You did good," she praised.

"Whoa, whoa, whoa! Hold your horses, Billie, he's not my man." *Yet,* a little voice in her head added. "We haven't known each other but a month and I'm not trying for a repeat of the Jonah episode." Her mouth twisted wryly.

"And you won't get one, either. First of all, he's six times the man that Jonah was. Y'all dated for like a year before you got busy and see how well that turned out," she sniffed. "Nick is down-to-earth and real, which is just what you need. Just because he doesn't have a bunch of worthless degrees doesn't mean he's not the right man for you."

"Excuse you, he has a degree. Two, in fact. He had an associate's degree in construction management when he went into the army. And when he got out, he'd earned enough credits for a bachelor's degree. Said it was a big surprise to him because it wasn't like he was trying for it, but he has it. And thank you for making me sound like a snot, which I'm not. I'm not snobbish enough to think that a man has to have an MBA before I'll go out with him, but I think there should be a commonality of interests," she said as she reached for her iced tea.

"Don't start making excuses before you even get serious with the man. You don't know what y'all have in common at this point. Although I think there's one thing you have going for you. *Chemistry,*" she said, leaning towards Dakota with a mischievous grin. "Y'all were giving off so much heat last night I thought you might burst into flame at some point."

The swallow of iced tea she had just taken went down the wrong way when she heard her sister's words. It was so close to what Nick had said last night she was stunned. Luckily, Billie was still rattling on about Nick and what a favorable impression he'd made on her. "Anyway, make sure you leave the office on time tonight. I have a surprise for you," she said mysteriously.

Billie's face suddenly looked pensive for a moment and she frowned. "I really like your friend, Toni. She seems like a really sweet person, real down-to-earth. I hate to say anything," she said slowly. She bit her lower lip and then blurted out what was on her mind. "I'm not hatin' or anything, but that big honkin' diamond she's wearing is a fake."

"A what?" Dakota asked breathlessly.

"It's not real. That setting is not platinum; it's either sterling silver or white gold coated with platinum. And that stone is a CZ, as in cubic zirconia, as in cheap miserable boyfriend. All that work I did for Tiffany's and Cartier was like a course in diamonds 101. I learned so much about jewelry it's like I have a loupe in my eye now, I can tell zing-zing from bling-bling across a crowded room. I don't know what you should do about it, but I'd keep an eye on that so-called fiancé of hers because something is not adding up."

"That's horrible," Dakota said glumly. "Now I'm going to have to start snooping and you know how I hate that."

Billie gave her a look that said, "Child, please."

"You know what I mean! When it's work it's fine, but when it's personal, it's awful. But I couldn't stand for her to be hurt. What am I supposed to do, sit around and wait until the other shoe drops?"

"Yes, Dakota, that is exactly what you have to do. Keep your eyes and ears open, but be ready to help pick up the pieces when this blows up and it will. These things always do. Just come home on time, tonight, okay?"

"Oh, sure," was her absent-minded reply. She had too much on her mind to really pay attention to her younger sister. She had just taken a big bite of a new way of thinking and she was hoping it wasn't too much to swallow.

In a mere week, Dakota had moved into her brownstone and all her belongings were exactly where she wanted them, thanks to Billie. Her sister had spent the rest of her vacation getting her things moved in and put away, due largely to her ability to charm, wheedle, bully and entrance men into doing her bidding. Now Dakota had the home she'd imagined, laid out exactly the way she wanted down to the last detail. There were even a couple of details she hadn't expected. When she'd made her last walk-through of the house she'd had to ask Nick about some odd little shelves that were positioned by the sunniest windows in the house.

She smiled when she remembered his sheepish reply. "Umm, those are for Cha-Cha so she'll have something to lie on while she looks out the window."

Dakota had never been so touched by anything in her life. She'd turned into his arms and laid a kiss on him that would have curled his hair if it hadn't already been in that state from birth. Smiling at the memory, she took a deep breath and made sure everything was ready for the night. She'd asked Nick to be at her house after the fashion show and she wanted to make sure that all her preparations were perfect. The living room and dining room were just right; all of her artwork was hung on the walls, her sofa and loveseat were looking plump and inviting, the cream-colored upholstery contrasting nicely with the colorful print pillows that were heaped about. There were candles on the mantel and the coffee table just waiting to be lit, the right music for seduction was cued up on the stereo and the wine was chilling in the refrigerator, along with a tray of appetizing foods to tempt the palate.

She checked the bathroom once more; the extra towels were in place, along with a big fluffy terrycloth robe hanging on the back of the door. It was a beautiful shade of Nile green that would look devastating on Nick. Her bedroom was exquisite. She had an antique bed that had been made for a very large man and his wife and it easily held a king-sized mattress. It was so high off the floor that she had a little set of steps to use, but it would pose no problem for Nick. There was a bouquet of roses next to the bed, which was turned back invitingly and the gentle smell of the lavender powder she'd sprinkled on the mattress cover scented the room. The quilt Meemaw had made was folded at the foot of the bed and a soft amber light glowed from the nightstand. The silk jacquard curtains were rosy pink to match the duvet cover on the bed, and the 1,200-count sheets that had been a Christmas present from Billie last year were a softer shade of pink. It looked very feminine and girly, but she had a feeling that Nick would enjoy it. She just hoped she'd enjoy the fashion show, for which she was about to be late.

She picked up her tote bag and started making a mad dash down the stairs, calling to Cha-Cha to stay off the bed. Carefully locking the door behind her, she got into her HHR, which looked brand-new again, and headed to the hotel where the fashion show was being held. This was a special event for charity, as Toni had stressed over and over. A friend of hers had designed a new line of clothing for all sizes with the emphasis on the larger ladies, and this fashion show would intro-duce the line to Chicago. It was a big, festive event and Dakota was as prepared as she was going to be. Before she'd left for her next modeling assign-ment, Billie had taught her how to walk, how to move her body as though she owned it and not the other way around. She could do all the turns, she could step out with confidence and no fear of falling because of the masking tape crossed on the bottom of her shoes, she could look like a super-model and even toss her hair seductively. But could she make it out of the dressing room? That was the only hitch in an otherwise perfect plan. She had found out at rehearsal that Toni's friend designed lingerie. She'd almost caved right on the spot, but the other models seemed so together and in control Dakota had no choice but to step up her game.

She parked the car in the parking structure beneath the hotel and took the elevator up to the ballroom level. When she got to the area designated for the dressing room, she was relieved to see that she wasn't late; everyone else was just getting there, too. She greeted the ladies by name and exchanged hugs with a few that she'd gotten to know in the last few days. Some were older than she, some younger, and most were bigger, but what they all shared was beauty and confidence. It was a noisy, happy group of buxom beauties that was going to take the town by storm that night. They were modeling loungewear, bathing suits and underwear, as well as some amazing nightwear. Dakota had three outfits to wear and since she was in the first group of models to go out, she found she got rid of her nerves right away.

Her first outfit was a deceptively simple violet

dress that came to the floor. It was Grecian-styled in front with a modest cowl neck, and it was sleeveless. But when she executed her first turn and the audience could see the back, the ladies in the audience gasped and applauded because the back was nonexistent, exposing everything right down past the curve of her back. It also had side slits up to her hips and it was obvious that this was an outfit made for seduction.

"I want that for my honeymoon," a woman said loudly.

Now the place was rocking. Her next ensemble was a bathing suit in gold Spandex that was also backless with a lace-up front that exposed her breasts. The built-in bra made her breasts look spectacular, and when she deftly removed the matching sarong, the high-cut legs of the suit made her luscious legs look even longer. The applause was deafening, but Dakota wasn't paying it any attention. She had to get into her last ensemble, the one that would end the show. The designer, a woman named Maggie Jones, had created a special outfit to close the show. "Since it's traditional to end most fashion shows with a bride, I made this bridal lingerie. It's your size and you'll look wonderful in it," she'd assured Dakota.

For the first time in a long time, Dakota felt absolutely gorgeous. The white corset was made of silk organza and trimmed with handmade Belgian lace. It had tiny white buttons in the front and tiny bows with silk rosebuds at the top of the garters that held up her sheer white silk hose with lace tops. There was a small flirty skirt around the edge that didn't conceal the white lace thong worn with the ensemble. And thanks to Billie's surprise, she had no fear about wearing the tiny thong in public. The day Billie insisted she come home early, she'd taken Dakota to a wonderful day spa and given her the works, manicure, pedicure, bikini wax, massage, facial and aromatherapy. She had a whole new appreciation of her appearance now. Her makeup was perfect and she knew she looked her absolute best. She put on the amazingly sheer matching robe and the stiletto-heeled mules that matched the corset and made her entrance with a bouquet of white flowers and a gardenia nestled in her hair, which was full of luscious-looking curls and waves.

When she appeared on the runway all by herself, the ladies went crazy. Dakota felt as though she could fly. She looked like a very happy woman who was about to greet her brand-new husband for the most special night of their lives, their wedding night. She felt elated, filled with excitement and triumph and yet, strangely melancholy. She made her turns, flashed a beautiful smile and left the runway to return to the dressing area. She had no sooner reached the backstage area when the voice that haunted all her days and nights called to her.

She slowly turned to see Nick standing there looking like something out of a dream. For one wild moment she was afraid she'd conjured him up out of her fevered imagination. She watched him walk towards her and she prayed it wasn't just a fantasy. He was so close to her now she could smell his cologne and he touched her, putting one big hand on her shoulder and tipping her chin up with his other hand. "Let's go home, baby. I got something for you," he said before kissing her gently on the lips.

"And I've got something for you, too," she answered. "Let me get changed and I'll meet you there."

"Hurry, baby." He leaned down and kissed her once, hot and sweet. "Drive careful, but hurry."

Chapter 8

Afterwards, Dakota couldn't remember how she got home. She must have changed clothes at some point, because she wasn't wearing the bridal lingerie anymore. She had on the same little blue dress she'd worn to the event, the one Billie had brought her from Italy. She was wearing the matching sandals and her toenails were still gleaming from her recent pedicure. She didn't remember parking the car in the driveway or even opening the front door. All she really remembered was Nick walking in the door. She was once again struck by how handsome he looked in his casual attire of jeans, pale-blue dress shirt and a navy sport coat. "You look wonderful," she said in a low voice unlike her usual manner of speaking.

"Not as good as you." He crossed the room to where she was standing and without any further conversation, he picked her up and headed for the stairs.

"Nick!"

"Yes, baby?"

"We're supposed to start downstairs," Dakota protested feebly. "I have wine and music and candles… ooh," she sighed as they entered the bedroom and Nick placed her in the center of the bed.

Nick locked his eyes on hers as he took off his jacket and hung it on the back of her vanity chair. It was followed by his dress shirt, which he unbuttoned while he kicked off his highly polished loafers. "We can finish downstairs, baby. But we're starting right here and now."

Dakota was mesmerized by the sight of his broad shoulders, his muscular arms and chest, which was covered in a thick mat of the same soft curls that graced his head. He was unbuckling his belt when Dakota rose to her knees, saying his name urgently. "Nick!"

He didn't pause in removing his pants, he just said "What is it, honey?"

"Close the door if you don't want Cha-Cha in here. And lock it," she said breathlessly.

Nick did as she asked and, when it was done, he turned around. He was naked, throbbing and ready for her, something all too evident from the massive erection he was displaying. He walked to the bed, saying, "Now it's your turn, Miss Lady."

Dakota, still in her kneeling position, reached for the straps behind her, but Nick stilled her hand. "Let me do it," he said in a deep, loving tone of voice. He lifted Dakota off the bed and turned her so her back was to him. He undid the straps and the zipper while she stepped out of her shoes. A soft sigh of pleasure escaped her lips when she felt his strong hands stroking the dress away from her body. It fluttered down to her ankles while Nick kissed the back of her neck, running his tongue down the sensitive skin until he touched the delicate bone at the top of her spine. She was now wearing only her strapless bra and a matching thong, so that Nick got his first look at her derriere, a view that brought him a lot of joy, to judge from the sharp intake of his breath. "Damn, baby, you've been hiding all this from me?" he moaned as he palmed the smooth globes.

He unfastened her bra and took a deep, shuddering breath as he put his hands on her bare breasts, squeezing them gently, then cupping them in his palms and tracing her sensitive, erect nipples with his thumbs. He turned her around to face him, smiling down at her. "I knew you'd be beautiful," he told her. "You're everything I knew you'd be." He put his thumb in the band of her thong and gently pulled it off, holding her so she wouldn't fall when she daintily stepped out of the flimsy garment.

Now she was standing before him completely nude, her silky skin glowing in the muted light of the room. It was an amazing moment for her. A few weeks ago she could barely stand to think of taking her clothes off in front of anyone, and now she was proudly putting herself on display for him. She wanted Nick to look at her, to continue to devour her with his eyes the way he was doing now.

"I want to see all of you, baby, every single inch. Damn you look good," he said as she moved so he could see her back as well as her front. "Kiss me, Dakota, I want to taste those sweet lips again."

Trembling with anticipation, their bodies made contact for the first time. The feel of his chest against hers was wonderful, but there was more to come. Nick's hands slid down her back to caress her hips and behind, and then he picked her up and put her back on the bed, lying down next to her. He kissed her again, a long, languorous kiss that went on and on as he stroked her breasts, continuing his exploration of her body. His hand moved down her firm, rounded tummy and stopped when he got to the apex of her thighs. He stroked her there and she parted her legs to allow a deeper caress, which he expertly and gladly applied. His middle finger found her wet and yielding to his touch while his thumb explored the most sensitive part of her.

Now his lips were traveling down her throat, past her collarbones to find her breasts. When his mouth, hot with passion, covered her nipple she cried out, calling his name. He answered her by intensifying his assault of the tender tip of her breast, coupled with his sensual exploration of her womanhood, which was hot, wet and throbbing just for him.

"Nick, Nick, ohh, Nick don't stop, don't stop," she moaned as her fingers gripped the linens.

The pleasure went on until she cried out again and he could feel her muscles clenching and unclenching and he knew she'd had her first climax. Only then did he still his motions long enough to put on the condom he had in the palm of his free hand. Dakota sighed in protest when he stopped touching her, but the sound turned to one of satisfaction when he lowered his body onto hers. He held his manhood in one hand, rubbing the tip against her and sliding it into her with excruciating tenderness. He took his time, entering her with reverence and control, letting her get used to the size of him. He was rock-hard and heavy with desire, and his strokes became deeper and faster, plundering her sweetness as she clung to him, screaming his name and digging her fingers in as another climax rocketed her into a universe of pure sensation.

He was braced on his elbows, sweat was glistening on his face and his body and the sensations he was experiencing were the most intense and sensual he could remember, but he didn't want to stop. He didn't want the feeling to end, even though the release would be earth-shattering. Suddenly, Dakota's hips starting moving in a new rhythm, matching him stroke for stroke but adding an unexpected suction that almost knocked him off the bed. Now it was his turn to cry out and her name was torn from his throat as a feeling of absolute euphoria took him over. He shuddered as he strained to ride out the incredible tremors that were rippling through his body. He wrapped Dakota in his arms and rolled over so she was on top of him and held her tightly until he could breathe again.

He had to strain to hear it, but the silence was broken by the sweet sound of her sigh. "I love you," she said softly.

Nick was more content than he could ever remember being. Dakota was still on top of him, but they were downstairs on her couch at last. The CD player was giving out the incredible sound of Johnny Hartman and John Coltrane, the rich scent of the Warm Spirit Paisley candles scented the air and Cha-Cha was inspecting the remains of their feast, trying to see if there was some scrap that had her name on it. Dakota had arranged a low table next to the sofa and they had fed each other while sipping champagne and kissing madly. The shrimp and smoked oysters were all gone and Cha-Cha wasn't fond of the fruit that was still on the tray, so she contented herself with a cherry tomato, which she knocked to the floor and chased through the dining room.

Nick was wearing the rich green robe Dakota had bought him and she was wearing a soft peach camisole with matching tap panties. It was so sheer she might as well have been wearing nothing at all, but she looked so delectably sexy he could barely keep from ripping it off and making love to her again. But since they'd already done that in the bed, in the shower, in the bed again and then on the sofa, he thought he'd better let her rest. Dakota stirred, although all she did was raise her body up so she could open the front of his robe and then nestle against him, stroking his chest while she sighed with happiness. At least he thought it was happiness. She'd confessed her love for him, which was a first, just like the robe he was wearing. He was trying to remember when a woman had done something like that for him but he was coming up short. Dakota was just one of a kind, something he'd already known.

"What's on your mind, baby? I can hear the

wheels spinning so I know you're thinking about something," Nick teased her.

"I'm thinking about making love. Can we do it some more? It was wonderful," she said dreamily.

"I'm trying to spare you, Miss Lady. I don't want you all sore and uncomfortable tomorrow 'cause then you'll be mad at me and I don't want that. Oh damn," he groaned as her hand wrapped around his manhood. "Dakota, baby, it's a good thing I had on a condom tonight because you'd be pregnant right now."

Dakota laughed at his outrageous statement, but she kept caressing him, holding him gently but firmly, moving her hand up and down as she contradicted him. "You sound mighty sure of yourself. Suppose I did get pregnant, what then? You'd run for the hills, wouldn't you?"

She squealed in surprise as Nick abruptly sat up and swung his long legs down, bringing her around to sit in his lap while he grasped her upper arms firmly. "You need to warn somebody before you do things like that," she fussed.

"And you need to quit playin'. If I was lucky enough to make a baby with you we'd get married and have the prettiest baby anybody ever saw. Did you think I was playing when I said I was going to make you mine?" Without waiting for an answer, he kissed her hard and fierce with an intensity that was almost punishing until his mouth softened and it turned into the kind of sweet, sensual kiss she'd learned to expect from him. He locked his arms around her waist and when they slowly pulled away from each other he looked completely serious. "Are you my woman?" he asked softly.

"Are you my man?" she countered, looking equally serious.

"You know I am," he growled.

"Show me," she said boldly.

"Stand up for a minute and I will." She stood while Nick took off his robe and spread it out on the sofa. "Take off your panties and sit down, baby. Sit right on the edge." He took a couple of the throw pillows off the sofa and knelt on them while he brought her legs over his shoulders. "Now try not to scream too loud," he cautioned and then bent his head to begin a long and intimate kiss that made her dizzy from sensation. His lips and tongue were bringing her to the edge of unreason with hot sparks igniting every part of her body. Her hips were pumping in sync with the stroking of his tongue and her fingers were laced in his thick hair as she was shaken by one massive orgasm after another.

She tried to hold it in, but the sounds of her release filled the room, she was screaming Nick's name again and again. He finally began to end her sweet torture, kissing his way up to her lips. She was trembling and glistening with a fine sheen of perspiration, and she clung to him while they kissed. Tears shone in her eyes and Nick kissed them away. "Damn, you're loud. I like that in ya, baby. Now, am I your man?"

"Yes, you are. And I'm your woman. Take me upstairs and I'll show you," she murmured.

And he picked her up and did just that.

A long time later, Dakota awoke. She was lying on something wonderful; it was soft and warm and she arched into it, craving more of the sensation. The warmth increased as she felt something enfold her, something that made her feel even more secure. Her eyes opened slowly and she realized that she was on top of Nick and her breasts were cushioned against his chest. His arms were around her and her head was nestled into the crook of his neck. Nick was awake, too, because she felt his arms loosen and his hands begin to move up and down her back. She didn't have on a stitch of clothing and she felt wonderful. She was tingly all over and when she moved, all of her erogenous zones throbbed. Everything they'd done the previous night came back to her in crystal-clear detail and a low murmur of contentment issued from her lips. She moved so that she was straddling Nick, but she didn't raise her head. She felt too comfortable, too safe and too loved to do much more than she was doing.

A deep laugh came from the depths of Nick's chest. "Good morning, baby. How do you feel?"

She took her time in answering, mostly because she didn't want to break the spell that surrounded the two of them. Finally she slid down his body a little, so she was resting her face on his chest, rubbing her cheek against the soft hair that felt so good to her bare breasts. "I feel wonderful, Nick. How about you?"

"I just woke up with my woman in my arms after making love all night. That's a pretty good start to any day," he said with gentle amusement.

"Are you hungry? I can make you breakfast," she said with a dainty little yawn.

"What I'm hungry for doesn't need to be cooked. And you don't need to get out of bed to fix it," he answered.

He moved his hips and Dakota could feel his erection growing. She giggled while she moved her own hips so she could feel more of it. She raised her head and braced her chin with her hand as she looked down at him with love in her eyes. "You're just insatiable, Nick. Are you never going to get enough?" she asked.

"Never in this world, baby," he said while gripping her hips. "And I seem to remember someone in this bed saying she wanted more. Said it several times, if I recall," he reminded her.

Dakota pushed up so that she was riding Nick, her body rising up and down with every movement of his pelvis. It was true; she hadn't been shy about letting Nick know how much he was pleasuring her and this morning was proving no different. In fact, her body was so attuned to his and so easily aroused by him that she was already feeling close to the edge. She looked down at Nick with eyes half closed from the passion he was stirring in her and said his name with the intense longing he excited in her. "Nick," she moaned, and his movements got faster and more forceful. Her back was arched and her eyes closed and the only thing she was aware of was Nick and how he was making her feel. After she rode out yet another shattering release she collapsed into his waiting arms and sighed his name, over and over.

"Nick, sweetheart, eventually we're going have to get out of this bed," she murmured.

"Yeah, I guess we are," Nick agreed lazily. "But not for a while. When we're old and gray and can't do this anymore, we gonna wish we'd done it more," he said with a smile.

"You have an excellent point," she agreed and sighed with repletion as he took her in his arms once again.

Chapter 9

The next few days were the most fun Dakota could remember in a long time. It was so wonderful having Nick in her life. They'd spent the entire weekend after the fashion show together and she'd laughed more than she had in months. When they finally got out of bed it was after twelve and they took a long shower together before she went downstairs to make him breakfast, something on which she'd insisted. She was touched to realize that he'd come downstairs during the night and cleaned up after their late-night repast, and was further impressed that he took the sheets off the bed and put them in the washing machine while she made him a brunch of eggs Florentine and a tender filet mignon. She was making biscuits when he brought the sheets down and stopped when she saw what he was doing.

"You made the bed?" she asked in surprise.

"Yeah, I did. It's just how I am, baby, I don't leave the house unless the bed is made and the bathtub is cleaned out. I've been called a neat freak before so don't hold back."

A guilty flush spread across her face as she thought about her own housekeeping. She was of the live-and-let-live school and if it wasn't crawling, she didn't worry about it. A local maid service had always served as a way of keeping the dust bunnies at bay, but obviously she was going to have to do better in that department if she was going to have a neat man in her life. "You want hash browns or grits?" she asked.

"How can you ask a Georgia boy if he wants grits?" he grinned.

Soon they were seated at the small breakfast table in the sunny kitchen and after saying grace

Nick took his first bite of her cooking. "This is good, Dakota. What kind of eggs are these?"

She flushed again as she told him they were called eggs Florentine. "I should have asked if you liked spinach," she said. "They're not too fancy are they?" She looked down at the poached egg in its bed of sautéed spinach with dismay.

"Dakota, look at my plate. Does this look like too fancy for you?"

He'd cleaned his plate and was still looking hungry. "I don't have a problem with trying new things as long as they're good," he informed her. "And if you don't eat yours pretty soon, I'm gonna take it. You worked me pretty hard and I'm a growing boy," he said, with not even a hint of shame.

They both laughed as she gladly let him have her portion. She had an extra biscuit to make up for its absence and smiled when he complimented them. "If I hadn't seen you make them I'd have thought my mother was in the kitchen," he said.

She poured him another cup of coffee as she thanked him. "My mother and my grandmother taught me pretty well. I don't cook as often as I'd like to, but I enjoy doing it."

"You can cook for me anytime, baby. What do you want to do today?"

"Everything," she said and leaned over the table for a kiss.

They did just about everything that weekend. First they went to Nick's house so he could change his clothes. It was the first time she'd been to his place and she was most impressed. It was a big brick home in the northern suburbs and had obviously been restored by his expert crew. The front door was mullioned panes of glass and when he opened the door, Dakota was blown away by what she saw. The circular entryway had a highly polished parquet floor with a round oriental rug and an antique table, also round. The living room was huge, with big windows that let in the sun. The floor in there was carpeted with rich cream-colored Berber and it made the room look even bigger. The walls were the same color as the floor and the woodwork was in its natural state, including the crown molding and the French doors on either side of the fireplace that led out to a solarium. The dining room would easily sit sixteen people and there was a built-in glass-fronted china cabinet that went from wall to wall, ceiling to

floor. The proportions of the rooms were magnificent; the only thing that was missing was furniture.

There was a large room that he used as a study
and in there was a computer desk, a sofa and
armchair and a huge plasma high-definition TV,
but not much else. The built-in bookcases that
lined one wall were virtually empty except for
business publications and a few family photo-
graphs. Dakota looked at Nick in surprise. "This
is beautiful, Nick, but why is it still empty? How
long have you lived here?"

"I know, I know. I need to get some furniture,"
he admitted. "But I've been taking my time about
it for some reason. I want to make sure I get all
the right stuff," he admitted. "I think I might have
gotten in over my head. I always know what I
want, but when I try to put it together it doesn't
always work."

"So is that why your apartment looks like…"
her voice faded away and she turned bright red as
she realized that she was about to insult his taste.

Surprisingly, though, he didn't take offense.
"Yeah, it's kinda out there. I was dating this
woman who had no more taste than I did and
together we made a mess of that place. I know

what I wanted it to look like, but the end result wasn't quite what I had in mind. But I'd spent so much money on it, I wasn't going to just get rid of the stuff."

They were in the solarium and while Dakota was admiring the windows, he made a startling confession. "I grew up with nothing. Paul and I didn't have even the basic things that make life easy, like an extra pair of shoes or warm coats for the winter. We just barely got by for our whole lives. So when we started making some real money, we started spending like big ballers," he said with a dry laugh. "We had the money to have anything we wanted and that's how we spent it. Clothes, cars, jewelry, whatever we wanted. And we wanted the best, too. Hell, we could afford it."

Once again Dakota's candor kicked in before her tact could make it to the gate. "But Paul doesn't have a bunch of gaudy stuff in his house," she blurted out, then covered her mouth and closed her eyes as she realized too late what she'd said.

To her relief, Nick just laughed. "That's 'cause Paul has Patsy and she knows how to decorate a house. She has real good taste, she knows how to put things together real nice. I guess it really takes a woman's touch."

Dakota raised her hand to volunteer her services. "I'll be happy to help," she offered. "I have excellent taste, thanks my mother, and I'm really frugal. You don't have to break the bank to make things look wonderful. If you know how to shop you can get beautiful things for next to nothing. I know how to get the best for less, trust me."

Nick smiled down at her. "I figured you would. Come see the rest of it," he invited. They toured the rest of the house, which had a big kitchen and state-of-the-art stainless-steel appliances, a breakfast room and pantry as well as a lavatory and laundry on the first floor. The upstairs had five bedrooms and two full baths, as well as a bathroom in the master suite. This room was furnished as well, although it had only a gigantic bed with a matching dresser and chest of drawers, as well as two nightstands. The bed was magnificent, high and huge with paneled head- and footboards. There was a thick brown jacquard cover and six big pillows in matching shams.

"This is the best bed I've ever seen in my life. Can I sit on it?" she asked in wonder.

Nick laughed and picked her up, settling her in the middle while she made a noise of enjoyment. "I'm going to love making love in this bed," she said shamelessly while he took off her little flats. She scooted up to the head of the bed and rested on the pillows, which felt fantastic. "Nick, we really need to christen this bed," she said with a seductive smile.

Nick sat on the edge of the bed and took her into his arms for a long kiss. Then he looked at her sternly. "We'll do that tonight, but right now I'm changing clothes and we're getting out of here."

He laughed as she made a mock pout and captured her lower lip in his mouth. "C'mon, baby, don't tempt me anymore. Let me take you out and show you a good time and then I promise you we'll break in this bed good and proper tonight."

Dakota leaned back into the big pillows and gave him a seductive smile. "Well, you haven't broken a promise to me yet, so I'll take you at your word."

"My word is my bond, Dakota. If I tell you something you can take it to the bank," he told her seriously. "And keep your little hands to yourself so I can get dressed," he added, just as she was reaching for him.

She stuck her tongue out at him and told him to hurry. "Or I can't swear that I'll behave."

"You can misbehave all you want tonight, baby."

The rest of the day was spent enjoying themselves. They went sightseeing with Nick pointing out places of interest like Wrigley Field, home of the Chicago Cubs. As they drove past the venerable stadium, Dakota asked. "Do you like baseball?"

"It's okay. I don't pay that much attention to sports."

"Really? You don't veg out on the weekends and watch ESPN? You don't zone out on Sundays and watch the NFL or NBA after church?" She couldn't keep the skepticism out of her voice.

Nick laughed at the look on her face. "No, I really don't. Sunday is for getting ready for Monday. Got to make sure I have everything in order to start the week," he said.

For some reason the words seemed like ones she would hear again. Her brow knit in thought but she was quickly distracted by Nick reaching over to rub her thigh. "You look good in shorts, baby. I thought you didn't like to show off those pretty legs."

She batted her lashes and said in a breathy voice, "I usually cover them up, but my man likes to look at them."

She was indeed wearing a pair of wide-legged walking shorts. They had cuffed legs and pleats at the waistline and she looked fashionable and sexy at the same time. With them she wore a close-fitting white tank top and cute little black-and-white flats. This and other flattering outfits were the result of her shopping spree with Billie and Toni. She loved the way the outfit looked on her body and the freedom she felt in wearing it. She also loved the feeling of the summer breeze on her bare arms after so many years of trying to cover up instead of show off.

The best part of her new look was in her earlobes, courtesy of Nick. He hadn't been kidding after the fashion show when he'd told her that he had something for her. Sometime during the night, after they'd made love for the third or fourth time, he'd gone to his sport coat on the back of the chair in her bedroom and taken something out. He called her name and said "Catch," casually tossing a small velvet box in her direction. Her breath had caught in her throat and when she opened the box she couldn't say anything for almost a whole minute.

"Nick…these are fantastic, they really are. I've never seen anything so gorgeous in my whole life, but I can't accept them," she said in a faint voice.

"Yes, you can. And you will. You don't need to be borrowing earbobs from your baby sister. Put them on," he told her, his eyes twinkling in enjoyment of her shock.

Dakota had shed a few happy tears at that point. On the night Nick had taken them out to dinner, she'd said something about being afraid of losing one of Billie's earrings. And he'd not only been listening to her, he'd remembered and gotten her a pair of her very own. A really *big* pair, at that. "Nick, these look like a carat each," she marveled.

"They're a carat and a half," he corrected her. "Put them on so I can see how pretty they look on you."

He was acting as though he'd given her a bottle of soda pop instead of the most expensive and fabulous jewelry she'd ever owned. She'd put them on and her eyes had teared up with happiness when she looked in the mirror.

She had jumped on the bed and hugged him, covering his face with kisses. "Nick, you're wonderful. You're so sweet and thoughtful. I love them and I love you for giving them to me. I'll treasure them always. But—" she bit her bottom lip. "Suppose I lose them? I'd be absolutely devastated."

Nick had cradled her in his arms and hugged her, kissing her teary lashes and nuzzling her neck. "They're insured. If you lose them, they'll get replaced. They look good on you, baby. You make them look good. You're really special, Dakota. I hope you know that."

She smiled as she remembered his sweet words. Touching her earlobe where the big diamond was resting gave her a little thrill that was duplicated by the warmth of his hand caressing her bared thigh.

"I want to show you off, Dakota. I want everybody to see me with the most beautiful woman in Chicago. Let's go out tonight. What do feel like doing?"

She thought a moment before answering.

"Well, we could go to a play," she said slowly. "Or we could go to an art gallery. That would be nice."

"Damn, baby, I said go out, not get educated. It's summer time in Chicago and you want to spend the night in an art gallery?" Disbelief tinged his voice.

Dakota laughed because she'd been messing with his head to an extent. "Well, honey, what do you want to do? We may not like to do the same things," she said cautiously.

"We don't have to. If we liked all the same things we'd be the same person. What fun is that? If you want to date yourself you can stay home on Saturday night and clip coupons. Differences are what make things exciting, baby. We can do some things you like to do and some things I like to do. That way we both get exposed to new things and that's how we grow into a real good relationship."

Dakota sat back and stared at Nick. Once again he'd caught her off guard. What he'd just said was worthy of Dr. Keith Ablow or even the great Oprah herself. Her face showed everything she was thinking and she felt her cheeks redden when he called her on it.

"I got you thinking now, baby! You're wondering who that handsome devil is next to you with all the million-dollar psychology. It ain't Dr. Phil, it's just me, Miss Lady," He laughed raucously, and then looked at her with warmth and affection. "Don't worry about this, Dakota. We've got everything we need for this to work out just fine."

He parked the Escalade at a strip mall that had a large farmer's market at one end. There was also a greasy spoon which was Nick's immediate target. "You like hotdogs?"

"I sure do," she answered.

"Good. These are great. Chicago-style, you'll love them. Then we can go to the farmer's market. I noticed you like a lot of fruit and vegetables and they have real good produce there."

When they were seated in the tiny restaurant, Dakota sniffed her 'dog appreciatively before eating. "Mmm! I love hotdogs, always have. I actually like them better than burgers. Better than a Philly cheese steak and that's sacrilege where I come from. I'm from Pittsburgh, not Philadelphia, but cheesesteaks are still the big thing back home."

"Do you like Reubens?" he asked. She nodded because her mouth was full. "I got the deli for you, then. We'll go there later on. I'd take you tomorrow, but Paul and Patsy want me to bring you over. It's Ebony's birthday and she's home for the weekend."

"Oh, that would be nice! I want to pick her up a nice present," Dakota said. "She's really working hard on that degree, going to summer school and all. I used to do the same thing," she said.

"Ebony's a good kid. You'll get to meet the rest of the kids this weekend. They were in Georgia the last time you were over," he told her.

Dakota didn't answer; she was sipping her root beer. She was staring at him, unaware that her expression was soft and full of love. He looked up to find her eyes on his face and smiled. "What's up? I got mustard on my chin or something?"

"No, nothing like that. I was just wondering why you never got married," she blurted out. She almost said what she was thinking, which was that he would make a wonderful, loving and attentive husband for some lucky woman.

Nick's expression changed. "Who says I never got married? I was married," he said succinctly.

Only Dakota's extensive experience as an investigator kept her face from showing her surprise.

"You were? I didn't know that," she said with studied nonchalance.

Nick shrugged. "No reason for you to know. I married my high-school sweetheart. Now, we had everything in common," he said sardonically. "We grew up country and poor, we both liked the same foods, same music, same everything. We knew the same people and shared the same hopes and dreams. The height of our ambition was to have a split-level house in Atlanta. That was big livin' to us. We wanted a split-level house and two kids, a boy and a girl. And two cars," he said, holding up two fingers for emphasis.

Dakota couldn't take her eyes from his. "What happened, Nick?"

"She had a slightly different timetable than mine, I guess. Got tired of waiting for me to get out of the service, but she didn't want to come with me, which she could have done. I wanted her to. I wanted her to see some of the world with me before the babies came. It just seemed like to me she'd want to be someplace besides old dusty south Georgia. But she wouldn't come." He took a long drink of iced tea. "So she started screwing her other high-school sweetheart and got pregnant.

I guess she figured the army took away my ability to count, because she tried to convince me the baby was mine. I was country, but I wasn't stupid. So I divorced her, left Georgia and never looked back. Me and Paul settled up here and that's it."

Dakota wanted to say something insightful and appropriate, but she couldn't think of anything that would sound right. But Nick wasn't finished. "Paul, now he's with his girl from back home and that worked out right nice. She came with him when he was in the service and she took every kind of course she could. She started out wanting to be a nurse, but she ended up a teacher. They have four of the nicest kids you'd ever want to meet and they're real happy."

She had to ask, it just came tumbling out of her mouth as though she had no control over her brain. "Do you think you'll ever get married again?"

Nick burst out laughing. "Baby, of course I will. I'm going to marry you. Haven't you figured that out yet?"

Chapter 10

It took the rest of the day for Nick to convince Dakota that he wasn't kidding. She'd jumped as though she'd been stung by a bee, and then she'd proceeded to knock over her root beer while he sat back and grinned like he was king of the universe. "That isn't funny," she hissed, sounding just like Cha-Cha in a snit.

"It's not meant to be," he said confidently. "You're my woman, I'm your man, and we're gonna get married sooner or later." She ignored him as she furiously mopped up the root beer with napkins. "You can't get mad at me for stating facts, Miss Lady."

"I'm leaving," she said hotly. She slid out of the booth and picked up her good Coach bag, frowning when she saw that it too had borne the brunt of the root-beer episode. She ungraciously snatched the handful of napkins he was holding out to her and continued her hasty departure, wiping her bag angrily. Nick easily caught up with her and took her arm.

"The farmer's market is that way," he nodded toward the other end of the strip mall.

"I really don't feel like looking at tomatoes right now, thank you. I feel like going home." She sounded like a pouty schoolgirl, but she couldn't help it.

"Why? Just because I spoke the truth? Are you upset because I didn't give you moonlight and roses and get down on one knee?"

Dakota opened her mouth to deny it, but the words didn't come out. She had suddenly remembered the night Jonah had proposed and it was indeed on a moonlight cruise down the Potomac with roses everywhere and a rather ugly ring that she never warmed up to. He had indeed given her moonlight, roses and the traditional kneeling pose and look how that turned out. Frustrated, she looked up at Nick with a frown. "It's not that. It's just that I take marriage very seriously and I don't think an open declaration in a dingy diner constitutes a proposal," she said angrily. "I'm not your plaything, Nick, and the sooner you learn that the better."

She tried to pull away from him again, but he was too strong and too quick for her. He had his arms around her and her head tilted up to his in a heartbeat. "Look here, Dakota, if anybody is playing it's you. Look in my eyes and see if I'm joking. You know I love you, woman. You know I want you and you know you're mine. What else can happen besides we get married? We're not kids and I'm not trying to go steady until we're fifty or some dumb mess."

She opened her mouth to make a heated rebuttal and found herself in a heated kiss instead. Nick applied his mouth and tongue to hers, and besides arousing her it gave her an odd sense that he was telling the truth. The kiss could have gone on forever as far as she was concerned, but a couple of comments from passersby reminded Nick that they were in a parking lot.

"Damn, baby. I'm sorry," he apologized. "I wasn't trying to put all our business out in the street," he said comfortingly. He kissed her on the forehead and they started walking towards the farmer's market. "I'm not too good at the smooth talk and the romantic stuff, I guess. Kinda out of practice," he admitted. "But it's going to be fine, Dakota, I promise you it is. You said I haven't broken a promise to you yet and I won't. You believe me?"

"Yes, but…"

"No! Not the 'yabbuts,' not from you, baby."

Dakota had no idea what "yabbuts" were, but Nick apparently found them highly amusing. He explained as soon as he got through laughing.

"I get that from my crew, or I used to. Same thing in the service. You tell somebody what to do, they don't do it and you call them on it. First thing out their mouth is, 'Yeah, but…' I got so sick of hearing it I started treating it like a disease. Anytime somebody starts making an excuse they go, 'Yeah, but…' Yabbut, yabbut, yabbut. My crew knows not to say that to me. I don't take excuses, I'm looking for responsibility."

They'd reached the entrance of the farmer's

market. "So try not to get the yabbuts, baby, it's a deadly disease."

Dakota was trying to think of a smart remark, but Nick kissed her again and she forgot whatever she was going to say. "It's going to be fine, Dakota. Better than fine, we're gonna have it all, wait and see."

She leaned against him, loving the way his hard muscled body felt against hers, despite her temporary angst. Maybe life really was that simple after all. You meet, you click, you claim each other and then you get married and have some happily-ever-after for a change. Maybe he was right about everything.

They shopped at the farmer's market long enough for Dakota to get a couple of cantaloupes, a honeydew, a seedless watermelon and everything else she'd need to make a fruit salad for Ebony's party the next day. Nick tried to convince her that it wasn't necessary.

"There's going to be a ton of food, there always is. You don't need to go to any trouble."

Dakota disagreed. "It's no trouble. I'm just cutting up some fruit. Besides, you can't go stepping up to somebody's house empty-handed and I don't want to bring something store-bought."

Nick looked down at the top of her head and pressed a kiss on her soft, scented hair. "Patsy is going to love you for this. She already likes you, but she's gonna love you for doing this."

After putting the groceries in the SUV, they went to a Bohemian area that was home to a number of cute little shops. She found a gift store with some lovely handmade stationery and some really nice leather journals. She bought the paper and a few journals for Ebony's birthday present. "Writers like to *write,*" she explained. "Even in this e-mail, text-message, cell-phone society, a real writer likes seeing words on paper. I think she'll make good use of these."

"Ebony thinks you hung the moon. You could give her a dollar-store trinket and she'd be happy as a pig in mud," he said dryly. He had selected a very stunning and expensive Mont Blanc pen for his niece, something of which Dakota heartily approved.

"Nick, she'll be thrilled. I had one once and I lost it at a book signing. I think someone wanted a souvenir from the author," she said ruefully. "It was a graduation gift and I never replaced it because I just couldn't spend that much money on myself for a pen. If you're really nice to me, I'll gift wrap it for you."

He leaned down to whisper in her ear. "I'll be more than nice to you for the rest of our lives if you let me."

Dakota's knees buckled a little and she felt that familiar tremor running through her body. Maybe life could be that simple. She uttered a fervent and silent prayer that this time it would be.

Things got a little chaotic after Nick brought her home. First she had to beg Cha-Cha's forgiveness for keeping her man away from her all day. Then she had to get some clothes together for their date. Nick said it didn't make sense for her to get ready there since she would be spending the night with him. So she had to pack a small bag with her cosmetics and accessories, as well as pick out two outfits, one for tonight and one for tomorrow. "Where are we going tonight, honey?"

"My favorite club."

Dakota waited for details but they weren't forthcoming. "Thanks, honey, that was helpful," she muttered. "How dressy?"

"Dressy as you wanna be, I guess."

Nick was sprawled across the bed with Cha-Cha, who was leaping and frolicking all over his long legs. He wasn't going to be a bit of help.

She was remembering two pieces of fashion advice, neither of which seemed really helpful. One was from the great Bill Blass, who'd said, "When in doubt, wear red." Then there was the adage about when you wanted to get attention, wear white. She had a better idea. When you're stuck, call your sister. She took her cell phone out of her pocket and punched in Billie's number, hoping that her wandering sister wasn't in some remote location where her signal had disappeared. Luckily, Billie answered on the third ring.

Dakota explained her dilemma, and Billie had the perfect answer. "Wear that white halter dress tonight. It's white, so it can go for dressy. It's cotton, so it will still feel casual. And it's hot so you won't have to wear hose. Tomorrow you can wear the red shorts with the matching tank and the multicolored sandals. Aren't you glad you didn't let Johnny take me back to the hospital?" she laughed.

Their brother had indeed wanted to return Billie

when it was revealed that he had another sister. He had wanted a brother, or at the very least, a football. "I would have never let him do it. I was the one who wanted a sister, remember that. Thanks for the advice. What have you been up to lately?"

"Same ol' same ol'. Photo shoots and runways, a couple of TV appearances, nothing too fun. I'm only doing this one more year and then I'm off like a prom dress. I want to start living in the real world," Billie said. "But let's not worry about little me. Let's talk about you and what you've been up to with ol' green eyes. Something naughty, I hope?"

Dakota was delighted to answer in the affirmative. "Very naughty."

Billie's squeal pierced Dakota's eardrum. "Go, Dakota! It's about time. Was it good naughty?"

"The best. And that's all you're getting out of me. If you're not in Bali or Monaco or Timbuktu in a month or so you should head this way. I'm having a housewarming and Mama and Daddy and Johnny will be here. Please come," she begged.

"And you know this! I'm not about to miss it, girl. Besides, I want to see you and Nick together again. You look so good and he's so sweet to you. The two of you give me hope, big sister. I've kissed enough frogs, there must be a prince for me out there somewhere."

They said goodbye and got off the phone. Dakota put her selected outfits in a garment bag and slipped the appropriate shoes into the weekender. When she emerged from the walk-in closet she was touched and amused to see Nick asleep with Cha-Cha lying across his chest as though she was claiming him.

"Chach, you know you're my main kitty, but that's *my* man, so you can forget about it. Now come on so I can get you some extra food and make sure your box is clean. You're going to be on your own tonight."

"Why can't she come with us?" Nick's deep voice made Dakota jump.

"You should let a person know that you're not really sleeping. You scared the life out of me. Cha-Cha will be fine on her own. She's used to being alone from time to time, Nick, she'll be okay."

His eyes were fully open now and when she looked at the bed two pairs of beautiful green eyes stared at her reproachfully. She burst out laughing.

"You know, you and Cha-Cha look a lot alike, especially around the eyes. That's so funny! But she's still not going. We'd have to take her food and her toys and her cat box and besides, she hates riding in the car, it would be a disaster. No. No way," she said firmly.

Thirty minutes later she and Nick were in the Escalade, on their way to his house. She was driving and Nick was the passenger with Cha-Cha purring happily in his lap. She was sitting up so she could watch the scenery and she seemed perfectly content, which annoyed Dakota to no end.

"She doesn't like that carrier, baby. I don't blame her. That's not a good place for her to be. Look at her, she's no trouble at all."

Cha-Cha actually turned to face Dakota and gave her a smug little grin accompanied by a little chirp of joy. "Okay, you ganged up on me and she got her way. I just hope you don't plan to do this when we have children, Nicholas DeVaughan, because that could get ugly," she muttered.

She didn't see the huge grin that Nick flashed when he heard her words. Whether she realized it or not, Miss Lady had just agreed to be his wife.

* * *

It took Dakota a little longer to get ready than usual, primarily because she had Nick helping. First, there was a long bubble bath in his big tub equipped with whirlpool jets. There was no way she could get into something that wonderful all by her lonesome, so the two of them bathed each other and discovered new ways to pleasure each other in the hot, fragrant bubbles. The jets were amazing, but even better was the hand-held shower attachment with different settings. She lay against Nick's broad chest while he showed her the different settings, trying each one out on her nipples. Every concentrated burst of water brought a new sensation until she was about to faint. But Nick wasn't having it. He coaxed her into a kneeling position and had her bend over at the waist. Then he directed the warm pulsing water at her most feminine parts and increased the pressure until she was once again writhing in pleasure and screaming his name.

She had her revenge for that sweet torture, though. She waited until he was letting the water out of the tub and they had rinsed all the suds away from their bodies. She was, for once, quicker than he was and when he'd put one foot on the thick bath mat and one foot in the tub, she made her move. She knelt down and took him in hand, holding him firmly while she guided him into her mouth. While he was groaning his pleasure she was treating him like the most delicious lollipop in the world, running her lips and tongue all over him and pulling him into her wet mouth until he was so hard he felt like steel. He roared her name and showed his strength and agility when he pulled her up out of the tub and hoisted her up until she could straddle his waist and slid down onto the bulging erection she'd created. He leaned against the granite-tiled wall and she managed to grab a towel rack to steady them while he took her to yet another level of sexual fulfillment. He could easily access her breasts while they were joined in this position and he took full advantage, fastening his mouth on one of her nipples that was as huge and sweet as chocolate candy. The combination of him in her and on her was so intense she felt as if they were doing this for the very first time.

The first climax was fast and glorious, leaving her breathing hard and trembling. The second one came quickly as the first tremors were slowing down. He gripped her hips even tighter and walked into the bedroom, where a bath sheet was already spread out as if he'd planned for a moment like this. He sat her down on the edge of the bed and he continued to pleasure her, pumping in and out as he moaned out her name. "Turn over, baby. Turn over," he said urgently.

She turned onto her stomach and knelt, bracing herself for what she knew was coming. He cupped her breasts and slid his hands down to her hips to anchor her against him while he continued to take her to the edge of an abyss where there was nothing but Nick, Nick, Nick. He was palming her butt with one hand while the other one was stroking her pearl. It was throbbing and wet and juicy from his loving and just when Dakota couldn't take any more of this erotic bliss, he began to lose himself in the hot moistness that was his alone. His back arched and every muscle in his body strained as the orgasm came. "Dakota, baby, damn baby, damn," he groaned over and over. He was still moaning her name when they finally collapsed on the bed and moved into each other's arms, spent and trembling.

When she could finally speak again, Dakota

took a great deal of pleasure in telling him, "Dang, you're loud. We're going to have to soundproof this room after the babies are born."

Nick laughed softly. He rubbed his face against her breasts, taking one in his mouth for a long, tender tribute before he said anything. He was caressing her, tracing a slow circle around her nipple when he finally spoke. "You're going to marry me, aren't you?"

"Yes," she said sleepily. "I sure am."

Chapter 11

As incredible as it seemed, they still went out that night. It was relatively early when they'd started getting ready, so when they woke up it was about ten and Nick still wanted to go. "I want to show off my fiancée. You still game, baby?"

And after a quick tepid shower, she was. She insisted on showering by herself this time, because she couldn't trust Nick to keep his hands off her. "You're a smart lady. Because if I get you naked again I'm not responsible for what happens. I'll use the other shower down the hall," he said agreeably.

Her hair was a hot mess, so she twisted it up into the all-purpose updo that Billie had taught her years before. It always looked good and it would help control her mane the next day. She was putting on makeup when Nick returned without a stitch of clothing on. He frowned when he saw her brushing on a touch of shadow. "Why do you wear that gunk? It doesn't make you look any prettier than you are," he said glumly.

"I like it. It makes me feel pretty. And it makes me look sexy," she replied. "You're not going to tell me you don't think Beyoncé is fine, or Mo'Nique or Jennifer Hudson. Or Oprah," she said pointing at him with her mascara wand.

"Who is Jennifer Hudson?"

"That gorgeous girl who was in *Dreamgirls*. The newcomer, the one with the powerhouse voice who won the Oscar," she said patiently.

"Oh. Yeah, they're all fine, especially her," he said appreciatively. "So what's your point?"

"They all wear makeup in public," she said patiently. "See? I'm all done. Don't I look pretty?"

Nick stared at her intently then scratched his head. She looked radiant, but not painted. Her face just looked smooth and flawless and her eyes were a little brighter and bigger. And her lips looked so juicy he wanted to suck them off her face. "Okay, you win. You look good, baby."

"Wait until you see my dress," she said with a wicked smile. While he disappeared into his cavernous closet, she slipped into the strapless bustier worn with the dress. The dress was simple and sexy with a halter neckline, a fitted bodice and a dropped waist. The skirt was flared and short, perfect for dancing. With it she wore open-toed shoes in taupe that had a three-inch heel and made her legs look a foot longer. It was another trick learned from Billie. "Never, under any circumstances, wear white dress shoes. Taupe makes your foot look smaller and your leg longer," Billie had told her.

She had a teeny little gold mesh evening bag that hung from her wrist and held only a mirror, lip gloss and her cell phone. "I'm going downstairs," she called to Nick and she suited action to words with Cha-Cha galloping ahead of her. "I wish you wouldn't do that," she sighed. "I keep telling you I can fall faster than you can run and I'm going to squash you one day if you're not careful."

She decided to get a glass of water while she

waited for Nick, but he appeared in the doorway to the kitchen before she could do so. Her smile lit up her face. "Ooh, I got me a pretty boyfriend," she said. "You look quite dashing, honey."

He really did, wearing a pair of light-colored slacks, a sage-green linen sport coat and an ivory silk T shirt. He also had on a thick gold chain around his neck and a gold bracelet on his wrist, but they accentuated his masculinity and didn't take anything away from the overall effect. In the meantime, he was looking at Dakota with his heart in his eyes. "You look too good to be going out, baby. Somebody might try to hit on you and I'll have to deal with him. You got enough money for bail?"

She gleefully held up her tiny purse. "Not a dime, so you'd better behave. Let's go before you sweet-talk me back up those stairs. Cha-cha, you behave yourself. Don't do anything to disgrace the family name," she said.

The cat was going to be confined to the solarium and the living room with her toys, food and cat box, so there was nothing she could destroy in her active play. She would probably fall asleep on the big soft towel and pillow Nick had provided her. They left by the back door, and, after Nick helped her into the Escalade, he drove her to their mysterious destination. It was a nightclub called Singin' the Blues. It looked rather unassuming on the outside, but the inside was really nice. There were big plush booths all around the room, a dance floor in the center and cozy tables that sat two or four people. Each table had a round glass top with a white candle in a blue holder in the center. Dakota liked it at once. It was intimate and kind of sexy and she saw what Nick meant about attire. The clientele ranged from college age to senior citizens and there was a wide variety of dress from very casual to very dressy. There was a menu with limited items, although Dakota wasn't at all hungry for food. It was the music she was curious about.

A place like this was bound to have some great music and in a very few minutes the MC announced the second set of the legendary bluesman, Donald "Road Dawg" Slocum. The audience erupted into applause. Any fan of the blues had heard of Road Dawg and they were primed for a great performance. Nick and Dakota were seated near the stage and when Road Dawg came out with his band, the applause was deafening. He launched into one of his signature tunes and was wailing back on his slide guitar. The music was transporting everyone in the room into a blues nirvana until he suddenly stood and motioned to the band to stop playing.

"Baby girl. Is that you? What you doing in Chicago, girl?" He held his hand out to Dakota and she blushed as she got up from her seat to greet him. "Y'all excuse me, but this here is my god-daughter, Dakota. I used to change her diapers when she was just a little bitty thing. Now look at her! Come gimme some sugar, baby girl and let me get back to playin' before these people want they money back."

When she made her way back to the table she sat down to a round of applause from the audience and tried to look innocent while Nick stared at her in amazement.

"You're just full of surprises, aren't you?" He had to lean over and whisper in her ear in order for her to hear him.

She just smiled and gave him a sassy wink.

The next day, Nick couldn't stop talking about their evening. They were in the kitchen making the fruit salad. Nick had gallantly sliced and seeded the smaller melons and he'd removed the watermelon from its shell, so all Dakota had to do was cut them up into bite-sized pieces, which she was doing rapidly while Nick was going on and on about spending the evening with Road Dawg Slocum. After the show, they'd gone to his dressing room and then on to an all-night eatery and had chicken and waffles with his band. "I haven't had that much fun in a long time, baby." Nick was straddling a chair and watching her deftly peel kiwi fruit and slice it into the mixture. "And I still can't believe you can sing like that. You been holdin' out on me, woman. What other talents do you have?"

Near the end of his set, Road Dawg, or Uncle Donnie as she called him, had brought her on stage to sing with him. "I taught her this song when she was a knee baby, I'ma see does she remember it." She definitely did, and they belted out "Mockingbird" together. Ike and Tina couldn't have done it better. Nick was absolutely astounded, but Dakota was nonchalant.

"My daddy wanted to be a bluesman. He never wanted anything else more in his life, except my mother. She was a singer, too. She'd actually done some recording and she was about to launch a career, or try to. But after Daddy got out of the service, Mama was pregnant with Johnny and it didn't make sense to try to chase after a dream when there were mouths to feed. So Daddy gave it up and went to work in the steel mills and never looked back. Mama didn't either. They still love to sing, but they sing in church now. And Daddy used to sing at union rallies and stuff. Honey, show that man a microphone and it's all over," she said fondly.

"We can all sing, but none of us pursued it. We all got interested in other things. Johnny is in labor law, big surprise, Billie is modeling and I'm writing. Billie has the best voice, though. She could get a recording contract in a heartbeat if she tried, but I don't think she will. She's about sick of the spotlight. She just wants to settle down and live a normal life."

Now she was slicing starfruit into the big bowl of melon, pineapple, blueberries, strawberries, kiwi and peaches. "Look my fingers are all pruny," she exclaimed, holding them up. "I think I'm about all fruited out. Can you put this in the refrigerator for me?"

Nick didn't hear her. He was still picturing how sexy she'd looked on the small stage and the powerful way she'd belted out the song. "That's why you yell so loud," he said, laughing at the affronted expression on her face. He got up from his chair and cupped her face in both hands. "That's a good thing, baby. I love to hear that sound. In fact, since you need to wash that fruit juice off you, I can take you upstairs and you can let out a shout or two before we leave."

"You need to quit, Nick," Dakota said, but she didn't sound like she meant it. "You get pretty vocal yourself, so you needn't talk about me." She was finished with the salad and gathered up all the peels and seeds and other refuse into a plastic bag. She wiped the counter off, sprayed it with an anti-bacterial cleaner and wiped it again. "But you know what? I like that sound, too. And we do have a couple of hours before we leave," she said, looking at his hard body as he put the salad away.

He stood up straight and closed the refrigerator door. He leaned one shoulder against it with his arms crossed. "So what are you saying, Miss Lady?"

"I'm saying...race you upstairs!" Dakota laughed as she took off for the bedroom, but Nick beat her there. "You cheated! You took the back stairs."

"Yeah, but you win, baby. Come here and see what I've got for you."

Dakota dissolved in laughter as he threw her over his shoulder and hauled her away for some hot soapy fun.

The party was in full swing by the time they arrived. It was held in the backyard with Paul manning the grill as usual and a long table set up with, as Nick had predicted, a ton of food. Ebony was elated by her gift from Dakota. "You haven't opened it yet," Dakota said with a smile. "You might be disappointed in the contents." Ebony had just hugged her tightly and thanked her again. "Whatever it is, I know I'll love it. This was so sweet of you, Miss Dakota."

Patsy was very happy to see the fruit salad, though, and graciously accepted it and the warm hug Dakota gave her. "Thank you so much," she said, handing the bowl off to her oldest daughter, Brianna. "I didn't have time to make one and this looks just delicious. Brianna, this is Miss Dakota, the lady Ebony's been talking about all summer. Dakota, this is Brianna. She goes to Princeton," she added proudly.

Dakota also met Wayne and Paul, Jr., the two handsome sons. Paul, Jr., was at Morehouse and Wayne was still in high school, something that was causing his father a lot of joy. "Just one more to get out of the house and then it's just me and my baby," he gloated as he turned over a slab of ribs that looked and smelled mouthwatering.

Dakota insisted on helping Patsy, who was equally firm in saying everything was under control. "You can just sit down and keep me company for a minute while I finish decorating the cake. My children won't stand for a bakery cake. I have to make a cake from scratch or they raise the roof," she said. "I'm just about done, though."

She was adding a fancy design with a pastry bag when she asked a surprising question. "So how did you like modeling in a fashion show?"

Dakota's eyebrows shot up in surprise. She wouldn't have thought that Nick would have mentioned it to anyone. Patsy saw her surprise and waved her hand. "Oh, you're wondering how I know about it. Leticia called me to spread the news," she said with a sniff. "She was at the show with some of her friends and she couldn't wait to broadcast it. Nosy woman. And just between us girls, she likes to keep up mess. I was so glad when Nick divorced her I didn't know what to do first, jump for joy or say a prayer of thanks, so I did both. She was just a horrible woman, just awful. I still can't believe that Nick gave her a job, but that's Nick for you. He's always doing things like that," she said absentmindedly. "Now it's done. I'm just going to let that set until it's time to bring it out. Would you like something to drink, dear?"

Most of what Patsy was saying was like a low buzz in Dakota's ears. She was still stunned by the news that Leticia Banks, Nick's office manager, was also his ex-wife. How did he happen to miss passing that little bit of information on to me? she thought furiously. Suddenly she felt ill. She was lightheaded and a little bit sick to her stomach. She wanted to go home right now, and she didn't see how she was going to make it through the party. More importantly, she didn't know how she was going to deal with Nick. How could he have kept this from her?

Chapter 12

Dakota managed to get through the party only because she was used to keeping her face straight and her emotions in check when she was dealing with something really heinous. The talent served her well on this occasion because she got through the afternoon without lighting into Nick and accusing him of all kinds of things. She was serenely calm and gracious to everyone and even though she was burdened with raging emotions, she held it in. And she didn't go for the jugular when they got in the car, either. She was quiet, yes, but that was because she was trying to think of the right way to say what she had to say.

"You're real quiet over there, Miss Lady. You tired?" Nick asked with real concern.

"No, I'm not tired. I'm confused. Yesterday I find out that you have an ex-wife and today I find out who she is," Dakota replied tiredly. She let that statement hang in the air for a moment before adding another comment. "I find it a little surprising that your ex-wife is also your employee. And I'm more than a little curious as to why you haven't mentioned it before." Her voice sounded tight and angry, and she couldn't have cared less because that's just how she was feeling.

Nick didn't seem to be ruffled in any way by her obvious hostility. He just nodded and said they had some things to talk about. "I wasn't deliberately hiding anything from you, Dakota. I mean, as much as we care about each other, we've only started getting to know each other. There're a lot of things we don't know yet and I figured it would come with time. I don't know a lot of things about you, but what I know, I know for sure. I know you're the best thing that's ever happened to me and I know we're meant for each other. All the rest of it doesn't matter," he said.

"That sounds really nice, Nick, but it still doesn't explain how your ex-wife happens to be your office manager. Wouldn't you like to know if my boss was my ex?"

"You don't have an ex-husband," he said in an infuriatingly calm tone.

"How do you know? I could be keeping all kinds of secrets from you." She stared out the passenger side window, unable to look at him.

"You wouldn't do that," he said in the same calm voice. "You're too honest and too impatient to lie. Lying takes up a lot of energy because you've got to remember who you told what lie to and then you have to tell a whole bunch of other little lies to keep everything straight. You don't live like that."

Dakota jerked her head around to glare at him. "I could be telling lies of omission," she said nastily. "I could just not be telling you something vital, which is essentially the same thing as lying."

"Is that what I'm being accused of? You putting me on trial for a, what did you call it, lie of omission? You got me convicted yet?"

Dakota went back to staring out the window, refusing to answer. They arrived at his house and she was about to open the door when Nick stopped her. "Hold it, baby. We're not going to bring anger into the house. We're going to clear the air out here and leave it out here, okay?" He waited for her answer and when he didn't get one, he continued speaking.

"Look, Lettie married her baby daddy, Lester, and they had another child after that. Lester was a lousy husband and an even worse provider. He was a drunk, a mean one who beat her and the kids. She didn't have a real good relationship with her family at the time and they said she was on her own 'cause she was stupid to get involved with him in the first place. She finally had to get away from him because he beat her so bad she was in the hospital for a week. She was scared he was going to kill her or one of her kids and she just picked up and ran. She went to her people in Danville, but it didn't work out too well. People say they'll help you out, but they don't really mean it. Well, maybe they mean it when they say it, but they don't know how it's going to affect them long-term and they can't handle it. Whatever the reason, Lettie was on her own again. She couldn't find a job, she didn't have a place to live and she and the kids were staying in a shelter when she got in touch with me.

"She was somebody who once meant a lot to me and I couldn't turn my back on her. I got her a place to live and gave her a job. It was supposed to be temporary, but she's real good at what she does, so I kept her on. Lettie is my office manager and she happens to have been my first wife, that's all. It may not be the most conventional arrangement in the world, but I'm not a conventional man. You don't have anything to worry about where she's concerned because once I'm through with something, I'm through. Period. I don't look back, I don't wonder what if, I don't try again. When I'm done, I'm done, and when I found out that she was pregnant with another man's child that was it for me. But I wasn't going to let her and those kids starve in the streets, either."

Dakota was looking at her hands, which were clasped in her lap. She didn't want to look at Nick because now she was really confused and ashamed as well. What Nick had done was the act of a man with a big heart and a conscience as well. How could she be mad at him for that? But she had to wonder if they were rushing into talks of marriage. There was so much they didn't know and hadn't talked about. Maybe they had just gotten caught up in some really good sex and they just weren't thinking clearly.

"Look, baby," Nick said softly. He gently used his long forefinger to turn her face to his. "We could have a computerized questionnaire made up and it would answer every question we could possibly have about each other from what your favorite color is to what size shoe you wear, but what would be the point? Even when you know somebody, or think you know somebody like the back of your hand, there's bound to be some surprises. Hell, I've known Lettie since I was ten and I wouldn't have believed that she'd sleep around on me. I've known you for a month and I know you'd never look at another man. So what does that tell you?"

Dakota finally said something. "It tells me that Lettie was an utter fool to let you slip away and that I'm not crazy. I overreacted because I was overloaded with too much information at once. I apologize, Nick. I'm going to work at not doing that again."

Nick was watching her, watching the setting sun turning the beautiful summer day into a warm dusk that tinged her skin with gold. "Don't apologize to me. I'm not perfect and neither are you. I've never seen perfection as a goal except on a project sheet and you're not a project. I'm not a project, either. We're just an imperfect man and woman who've been lucky enough to find each other. Can't we start from there and take it one day at a time?"

"Okay, Nick, take me in the house now because I'm about to cry and your neighbors will think you're beating me or something," she sniffed.

Nick laughed out loud but agreed that he was tired of being in the car. He got out and came around to her side to open her door and held out his hand to help her down. Suddenly she was wrapped in his arms for a long and much-needed hug. "You're fine, Miss Lady. We're gonna work this out, just like everything else."

Dakota held on as long as she could, then looked up at him with a question in her eyes. "Is this our first fight?"

"I wouldn't call it a fight, exactly."

"Good. I don't want to fight with you, Nick."

"I don't want to fight with either, Dakota. I do want to get a massage from you, if you have one to spare. But I definitely don't want to fight."

"You've got yourself a deal, sweetie."

That night, Nick had yet another surprise for her. It was spread across the bed when she went into the bedroom. Nick was downstairs playing with Cha-Cha and Dakota had come upstairs to see what he had that could be used for massage oil. Her eyes widened at the sight of the long violet gown she'd modeled on Friday. Once again, he'd done something really sweet for her. Her eyes got teary as she thought about all the ways he expressed his love for her without words. He found her sitting on the bed, holding the gown with tears trickling down her face.

"Dakota, what's the matter? I thought you'd like it," Nick said.

Cha-Cha proved she hadn't totally deserted her owner by jumping on the bed and going to Dakota, standing on her hind legs to examine her face anxiously. "I'm fine, sweetie." She leaned down to nuzzle her cat and wiped her eyes with the back of her hand.

"You're just so sweet I can't stand it," she sniffled. "You know, I never even asked you how you knew about the stupid fashion show and you show up to support me and then you bought me this beautiful gown and I just don't deserve you."

Nick looked as though light had dawned. "Billie told me about the show and your friend Toni got me backstage and whatnot." He came over to the bed and stretched out, pulling his woman into his arms. "You looked hot, baby. You were the prettiest thing out there and you were walking like you'd been doing it all your life."

Dakota gave a weak laugh. "That's all thanks to Billie. She drilled me for a week before she had to leave."

"Dakota, I need to ask you a question that you might think is kinda personal because it is. But I need to know, is it about time for your cycle?"

She froze in his embrace and he could tell she was doing some mental calculations. "Yes! Yes it is. I should start day after tomorrow. I forgot to warn you honey, when I PMS I'm like a crazy woman. It lasts for exactly twelve hours in which time I'm the most whiny and miserable person on the face of the earth. And for some reason I can't keep it in my head for twenty-eight days that it's going to happen again. Every month it's a horrible surprise. I endure a half day of utter misery and two days later it's like 'Oh, that's why I was so evil.'" She gave him a bashful smile. "I guess this is one of the things we're learning as we go along, huh?"

Later, Dakota was making good on her promise of a massage. Nick was lying face-down on the bed, stretched out on another bath sheet. She was straddling him and they were both naked. His skin was still warm and moist from the shower and she was using some lightly fragranced oil that she'd found in the bathroom. She poured big drops of it in a neat row down his spine and applied a little more to her hands, rubbing them together before using the palms of her hands to smooth the oil into his skin. When she began the movements of the massage he released a long breath of relaxation.

"That feels good, baby. Thank you."

"I'm happy to do this for you," she murmured. "I haven't told you this, Nick, but I was engaged before I came here. I met this man named Jonah Kittridge. He was from upstate New York and he was a lobbyist for the dairy industry. Lobbyists are interesting people, if you like that sort of thing," she said offhandedly. "Anyway, he was at a book party that was being given by my publisher and we hit it off. He was handsome, charming and he had really nice teeth, which I found out later were very expensive caps. But that's irrelevant," she said, mostly to herself. "Anyway, he had a law degree, an MBA and a Porsche and he wined me and dined me and took me to the symphony and the ballet and all sorts of pretentious affairs. And eventually we got really serious and he asked me to marry him. With moonlight and roses and vintage champagne," she added.

"Then he started in on me. Didn't I think I should cut my hair, and shouldn't I get highlights? Did I really need that dessert because after all, I wasn't getting any smaller? Couldn't I work on my laugh a little, because I sounded like a barmaid instead of a respected journalist and author? Shouldn't I start going to the Presbyterian church which had much more status than the little A.M.E. church I'd been going to for years? That kind of thing was his specialty," she said as she continued to knead Nick's warm, smooth shoulders and back. "The weight was his favorite target, though. He said being 'bootylicious' was fine for some video tramp, but not what he wanted to see walking down the aisle to take his name in marriage. He didn't want to see us in *Jet* magazine looking like Jonah and the whale, he said."

Nick was trying hard not to explode with the rage he was feeling. He wondered what it would feel like to put his hands around the creep's neck just for a few minutes. Dakota was still talking in the same calm, measured voice. "But I was liberated from that debacle by the most welcome distraction. He found some little girl who had just graduated from Sarah Lawrence and who had a much better pedigree than mine, and once he found her, he dropped me like a hot rock. She weighed about ninety-five pounds soaking wet and she was much easier to manage than I ever was. I thought I was brokenhearted, but I wasn't really. I was mad as hell at myself for getting involved with a chump like him, and I really questioned my judgment for a long time. I'm supposed to be pretty smart, but apparently I have the emotional IQ of a tree stump. I didn't trust men and I didn't like them too much, either. And I wasn't really crazy about me, either."

She didn't say anything for a while; she devoted her attention to giving him the best massage he'd ever had. "I decided that what I needed was new surroundings so I took the job with the *Herald*, packed up my computer and my kitty and headed to the Windy City. And I met you, and Toni and my sister came and snapped me out of my mope and guess what? I'm happy, Nick. I'm happy with me. I walk around the house naked all day long if I feel like it and I love what I see in the mirror. I love my hips, I love my breasts and I love my booty. I have a good strong body that takes me where I need to go and I'm quite proud of it now.

"But you know what really makes me happy?" She stopped rubbing and lay on him, stretching her arms out and twining her fingers with his. "*You* make me happy because you complete my soul. I'll never meet a better man if I live a lifetime. I'm a very lucky woman, Nick. I love you."

They lay without speaking for minutes, until Nick began gently to roll over so he could put her where she belonged, next to his heart. "You're an amazing woman, Dakota. You're smart and beautiful and kind and if I ever meet the sap who let you go I'm going to shake his hand and thank him kindly for doing the single most idiotic thing he'll ever do in his life. I knew when I met you that I was the man for you. I was the one who'd give you the only thing that was missing in your life, the love you needed. And you're going to get all you can handle until the day I leave this earth."

She was just about to burst into big ol' tears when Cha-Cha decided to join them with a loud purr and a particularly spectacular leap onto Nick's naked thigh. "Damn!"

"I told you to keep that door closed, didn't I?" Dakota was giggling madly and the only way Nick could shut her up was to kiss her senseless, as usual.

Chapter 13

The weeks flew by and Dakota couldn't remember a time in her life when she was any happier. Nick was everything she wanted in a man and a mate. He was loving, attentive, caring and he made her feel so desired it was like she was a different person with him. There were only two little things that she found disturbing about their relationship. One was the fact that she had discovered that Nick was a world-class workaholic. Even though he'd devoted himself to her at first, as the weeks went by, his tendency to put work above everything else came out. If Nick was involved in a project, he was in it up to his ears until it was over. Period. If he was late for a date, or missed one altogether, his work was always the culprit. The first time it happened she didn't know how to feel about it so she sat him down for a talk. There was no point in her getting upset about it if he didn't know how she felt, she reasoned, so she put all her cards on the table.

They had tickets to a play and she was all dressed and ready to go, waiting for Nick to pick her up. She waited for his knock at the door to no avail. She waited even longer for him to call her and tell her he was running late, and when that didn't happen, she called him on his cell phone and got his voice mail. Two hours after the curtain time, he finally arrived at her door, still in his work clothes. She was beyond angry at this point, she was just livid. She'd changed out of her sexy silk dress and heels and stood in the doorway wearing a pair of ratty shorts and a T-shirt. "What are you doing here at this hour?" She stared up at him with a frown and her arms crossed waiting for his answer.

He didn't give her any of his usual charm, to her surprise. "Look, I know I'm late, Dakota, but it couldn't be helped. Ran into some problems at that new complex and I had to stay there until they were taken care of. I'll make it up to you," he said as he walked past her into the immaculate living room. He looked at her pristine cream furniture and frowned. "I can't sit down looking like this. I'll mess up your stuff. Let me get cleaned up first," he mumbled while taking off his work boots. Without another word he went upstairs to the bathroom.

By now she had a couple of changes of clothing at his house, along with toiletries and hair care supplies, and he had the same things at her place. It wasn't unheard of for him to take a bath and change clothes, but it certainly was untimely, as far as Dakota was concerned. She sucked her teeth angrily and followed him up the stairs, prepared to tear him a new one. He was standing in the bathroom butt-naked while he watched the hot water fill the tub. Cha-Cha was sitting on the sink talking to him in a series of purrs and little yips when Dakota entered the room. Nick stepped into the tub and sat down, issuing a deep sigh of relief. "Damn that feels good. I've been at work since five-thirty this morning, baby."

It was after ten, Dakota realized with a pang. Regardless of whether or not he'd stood her up, Nick had worked an incredibly long day, something he did all the time. She went to the glass fronted armoire in the corner of the room and got a big jar of scented bath salts out. She went to the tub and knelt down next to it, pouring some of the aromatic salts into the water. "Nick, I'm not going to pretend that I'm thrilled to have missed that play. I may hold it against you indefinitely," she said with a crooked little grin. "But I have to tell you, honey, you work too hard. Way too hard."

Nick sighed in pleasure as she swirled the soothing minerals into the hot water, releasing a scent that was redolent of pine and balsam. "Dakota, I'm a working man, plain and simple. If I don't work, I don't make money. If I don't make money, I can't afford to live like I want to live. I can't handle not having money in the bank, money invested in case something happens where I can't work or business falls off. I have a lot of people depending on me. I got married men with families on my payroll and I'm responsible for them making a living. This ain't a hobby, baby, this is how it is. If you can't handle it, you need to let me know now," he said in a serious voice she'd never heard before.

Dakota didn't answer him right away. She was taking handfuls of water and pouring them over his big shoulders, watching the rivulets trickle down the broad chest that brought her so much delight. "Hand me that loofah," she said as she reached for a bottle of bath gel. She squeezed some of the thick green substance onto the loofah and made a soft lather before applying it to his back. Rubbing it up and down his spine in circles, she smiled as he expressed his enjoyment of her ministrations. Finally she began to speak.

"Nick, I can certainly appreciate your work ethic. You've built a great company and you do amazing work," she said. "And I know you did this all on your own. Nobody handed it to you and you're very wise to keep your eye on the bottom line. You have a sense of responsibility that's quite admirable. A lot of business owners get the business up and running and then they act like it's going to run itself, like they don't have to see to the day-to-day operations and that's when they go bankrupt," she added. She was thinking as she was speaking and it was plain from her thoughtful tone of voice. Nick picked up on it at once and prodded her to continue.

"But?"

She looked at him quizzically. "I hear a 'but' coming, baby. You're saying all these things like you understand, but there's a condition in there somewhere," he said dryly.

Dakota blushed and leaned over to kiss him. "You know me too well," she admitted. "All I'm saying, or trying to say is that you work too hard. You have your brother as your partner, you have project managers and site managers and all these other folks that you pay good money to, why don't you let them do what they're supposed to do?"

Nick kissed her back, but he didn't relent. "They're supposed to do what I tell them to do. And that means I have to keep my eyes on everything that has my name on it. Bottom line, Dakota, it's my company and my name on the line. I'm not going to lose everything I've worked for by standing on the sidelines and letting things go to hell while I'm off playing. You should understand that better than anybody, hard as you work."

Dakota continued to rub the loofah sponge over

his shoulders, and then down his chest when she thought about his words. She had always thought of herself as a workaholic, but she was a rank amateur compared to him. When she was writing a book, for example, she spent a lot of time researching it before she started writing. A lot of interviewing and a lot of legwork had to be done before she could even set down an outline. Even when she wasn't working on another book, she did mainly investigative reporting at the paper and she was better able to control the flow of her work. Dakota liked to work early in the morning when her mind was its most nimble and she got up at five without fail Monday through Friday. She wrote her copy then, and now that Nick was spending all this time working, she found herself working in the evenings, too. But she still managed to find time to spend with Nick and she felt that if he tried a little harder, he could do the same for her.

"Yeah, but…" The words died in her throat as she realized what she'd just said and she dissolved into laughter.

"Well, you gotta watch your time," she returned pertly. "I don't want all of your time, but I have to have some of it. We won't make any more weekday dates, but I want us to be together on the weekends. Can you agree to that at least?"

Nick didn't answer right away; he was staring at her intently. Suddenly he put a wet soapy arm around her and pulled her close to his body for a long, passionate kiss. "Dakota, I don't want to lose you baby. I'm going to do my best to keep all my weekends open so we can be together. I can't make any promises on the weekdays, but the weekends are all yours."

"I only need one weeknight from you. Remember that award I'm getting? That award for journalism? You promised to be my escort, remember? It's on a Thursday night; will you be able to make it? It's not for a month, so can you pencil it in?"

"You know I will, baby, I wouldn't miss that for the world. I'm proud of you, Dakota, and I can't wait to see you up there getting your due." His expression changed and he looked lustfully at her now-wet T-shirt clinging to her delightful breasts. "Since you're already wet, why don't you get in here with me?"

Dakota started to protest, but she looked at Nick's long, muscular body and began removing her wet top. "Why don't you let out that water and turn on the shower? I think there're some parts I missed," she said with a sultry giggle.

Nick did so at once, flipping the lever that controlled the tub stopper with his toe before turning the shower on. In seconds they had drawn the pink shower curtain and it was just the two of them wrapped up in each other and a cloud of fragrant suds. "I'm not going to miss even a little bit of you, baby. I'm going to get it all," he vowed. Her only answer was a moan of contentment.

The other thing that made her uncomfortable about her new love with Nick was the presence of his ex-wife in his office. Until she'd found out that Leticia was his ex-wife, she'd just thought the woman was kind of nice-nasty, a person who said all the right things without meaning a single one of them. She was always polite, even cordial to Dakota, but her bright smile never matched the calculating look in her eyes. When Billie was in town she'd commented on it to Dakota. They'd gone to Nick's office and while Billie was taking a tour of the impressive space, she'd given Leticia a long appraising look, but she didn't say anything until they were on their way back to Dakota's house. That's when she'd turned to Dakota and made a pronouncement with a serious face.

"I don't trust that woman in Nick's office. You need to watch your back around her," Billie had said frankly.

At the time, her words had surprised Dakota. "His office manager? Oh, she's worked for him for a long time, but she's okay. She's not a really warm person, but she's friendly enough," Dakota had replied. She'd been concentrating more on the traffic as she drove and she wasn't really heeding her sister's words.

"Dakota, listen to me, I know what I'm talking about. I was watching her when you and Nick were talking. Every time he looked at you and especially every time he touched you, little flames would shoot out of her eyes. And when he called you baby and kissed you goodbye I thought that fake ponytail of hers was going to fly off her head she was so mad. Her face turns this ugly color every time you come into her eyesight, how come you never noticed that?"

Dakota had given a little laugh and assured Billie that nothing was going on between Leticia and

Nick. "They work together, that's all it is, Billie. How would it look if I got jealous of every woman who worked in his office, or every woman he came in contact with? That's just nuts, little sister."

Billie made a face. "I didn't say anything was going on with them, I'm just saying that the woman doesn't like you. And she does like Nick. Any fool can see that she has some inappropriate feelings about the man. She's real territorial and it's not because she's a dedicated employee. She wants that man. I work with high-strung beauty queens all day long and I know how women think and act. You've lost your edge because you deal with men all day and you're so busy scouring the underbelly of crime in America you've forgotten some basic girl stuff. All I'm saying is keep an eye on that heifer."

These words went in one of Dakota's ears and breezed out the other side. She was sure her younger sister was overreacting to the other woman, that is, until she found out that Leticia was Nick's ex-wife. That's when she had to admit that there might be something more to what Billie was saying. She was tempted to call Billie and run it past her, but decided against it because Billie would have been back in Chicago on the next plane getting all up in Dakota's business. She and her siblings had always been close and Billie was overly protective of anyone she loved. No, it was best that she keep her turmoil to herself. Besides, if it was true, it was all wasted effort because no one could come between her and Nick. He made that quite plain every time they were together. Yes, he worked incredibly long and hard hours, but when he was with her, she was the only thing that mattered.

She had to remind herself of that fact the evening she came by Nick's office to pick him up for their Friday night date. They were going to have a quick dinner and attend a set at Singin' the Blues. Then they were going to a nice secluded inn for the rest of the weekend. Dakota was wearing a new dress, one she knew Nick would love. She was also wearing sexy heels and a cloud of Nick's favorite fragrance. Her hair was perfect, as she had just left the salon a few hours earlier. She couldn't wait to see the look on Nick's face when she walked into the office. Smiling in anticipation, she opened the door and went directly to Nick's private office where she was stunned to see Leticia sitting there with an evil smirk on her face. She nodded briefly to the other woman before greeting Nick. She actually didn't have a chance to say anything because Nick got to his feet immediately and came around the corner of his desk to embrace her.

"Damn, you look good, baby. Let me go wash my hands and we can leave. I've been shuffling paper all evening and they feel dry and dusty. I'll be right back," he said as he kissed her forehead.

Leaving the two women alone in his private office, Nick went to the washroom. Dakota didn't say a word, she just took the seat that Nick had vacated. Resting comfortably against the high, wide back of the custom-made leather swivel chair, she gave Leticia a measuring look without a hint of a smile.

"Working kind of late, aren't you?"

Leticia gave her a cheeky grin in return. "I work as long as Nick wants me to whenever he wants me to. I've been with him for a long time and I know what he needs and how he needs it better than anyone. You might want to remember that, Miss Whatever. I'm here because Nick wants me and that's not going to change anytime soon so you need to get used to it."

Dakota could feel pure fury stiffening her spine but before she could respond to that audacious statement Nick returned. He had not only washed his hands, he'd freshened up totally and had even put on a fresh dress shirt. "Baby, can you put these cufflinks in for me?"

He held out his arm to Dakota who obliged him at once. "Lettie what are you still doing here? I told you to leave two hours ago," he said without even looking at her.

"I was just trying to get caught up on some files," she said with a slight pout in her voice.

"Well, lock up when you leave. Have a good one," he said, still staring down at Dakota. He leaned over and whispered in her ear, "You look good enough to eat. Are you sure you want to go out tonight?"

"Maybe not," she said with a smile. "What did you have in mind?"

He whispered in her ear again, making her giggle madly and totally forget the other woman was in the room. "You've got a deal, sweetheart. Let's go."

Leticia watched them leave. They had both forgotten she was there, that much was obvious. But all that was going to change, and real soon. She'd had just about enough of being ignored and she knew just what to do to change the status quo. *Enjoy it while it lasts, Miss Thang. Because it's not gonna last much longer,* she thought.

After she was good and settled into her new home, Dakota threw a housewarming party for her family and friends. Her parents and her brother came to Chicago to visit and Billie was able to attend the housewarming as promised. It was lots of fun, with all her new friends from work, Paul and Patsy and even a couple of girlfriends from D.C. Everyone fell in love with Nick, especially her father. The two of them were as thick as thieves and her mother was the one who pointed out the reason for their instant friendship.

Lee, Dakota's mother, was a beauty, and it was easy to see where Dakota and Billie got their good looks. She was a rich mahogany with startlingly white hair worn fashionably short. She was full of figure like Dakota and all her curves were still in the right places. She was watching the two men sitting on the deck behind Dakota's house and shaking her head. They were both drinking beer and puffing away on huge Dominican cigars and laughing about something. "Honey, I hate to tell you this, but they're just alike. Most women fall for men just like their fathers and you're no exception."

Dakota had contorted her face in dismay, and Lee just laughed at her. "What did you tell me about his clothes?"

"Mama, his closet is like a warehouse! In my entire life I've never owned as many things as he has in there. And a lot of them still have the price tags on them! He has shoes, belts, ties, sweaters, suits, you name it, and it's in there. Not to mention the jewelry. Thank God he doesn't wear it most of the time, but there's a couple of diamond pinky rings in his jewelry box." She shuddered delicately at the thought of all the clothes her future husband possessed.

"Honey, you don't remember this, but when he was younger, your father was worse than that. And he had some outrageous stuff, too. He's actually toned it down over the years."

Billie and Dakota looked at each other and laughed because their father was still known as a snappy dresser who liked suits in unusual colors and silk vests and ties in outrageous patterns.

"It's because they grew up poor, honey. After a while, when they internalize the idea that nobody's going to come and take it from them, they'll calm down. But acquisition is a real big deal for them. Now that he has financial security it's important to him to have *things,* the things he couldn't have when he was growing up. Once you start having babies, it'll stop because all his focus will be on the children. You're going to have to stop him from spoiling them rotten, though. There's a real sweet streak in your Nick. He likes to shower you with love and he's going to drown those kids in the same emotion. You're going to have to be the disciplinarian," she said affectionately.

"I'm very happy for you, baby. You've done very well for yourself. I have to tell you, I couldn't stand that Jonah. I was so glad when you got rid of that leech! Nick is a totally different kind of man, though. That's your soul mate, Dakota."

Her brother Johnny was also very favorably impressed by Nick. He was still angry with himself over recommending a crook like Bernard Jackson to his sister. "I put some people on it, Cookie, but by the time they found out where he was hiding out, your man had already dealt with it." Johnny

was cautious by nature, especially after what
Dakota had been through, but Nick made a huge
impression on him. Johnny was about six foot
three and broad-shouldered with his mother's
coloring, and he was as handsome as his sisters
were pretty. He wore a goatee and kept his head
shaved, which gave him a debonair, sexy appearance but he was still single and not really looking.
His work took **up** too much of his time.

The weekend visit had been wonderful and
Dakota had been sorry to see it end, even though
her parents' visit had curtailed her time alone with
Nick. She and her father had gone out on Saturday
morning so he could see the neighborhood, and he
had to give her his opinion of her future husband.
Boyd Phillips was an imposing figure. He wasn't
overly tall, only about six foot one, but he com-
manded attention and respect wherever he went.
He was a much-sought-after speaker and motiva-
tor and he could accomplish anything he put his
mind to. He'd raised his children to have the same
attitude towards their goals.

"Sweetie, I have to tell you I was surprised by
your choice of a husband. Very surprised," he said
in his most serious voice, the one he used when he

wasn't pleased with something. "I was surprised that you had the good sense to get him after that limp noodle you brought home last time," he said with a loud laugh.

Dakota gave his arm a playful pat. "Daddy, don't tease me! You know how sensitive I am."

"Okay, baby girl, I'ma leave you alone. But I think you've got yourself a real good man. He's smart, he's tough and he knows how to take care of what's his. He's got a good work ethic and he'll be in your corner all the way. You'll never have to worry about him because that man is devoted to you. He appreciates you and he's going to treat you right. You didn't ask, but you have my blessing," he added with a glint in his eye.

Dakota's face flamed up. She hadn't consulted her parents about marrying Nick, figuring that at thirty-three, she was supposed to sink or swim on her own. Hoping she hadn't hurt his feelings, she tried to explain, but he waved it away. "Nick talked to me like a man, baby girl. The night we got here he asked if he could have a word and we did. Like I said, that's a good man."

Nick was a good man, and more importantly, he

was her man for life. She just couldn't imagine anything that could come between them, although Leticia seemed to be trying her best. It had gotten to the point where she called him only on his cell phone because there were a few too many times when she'd left a message on his voice mail that he said he never got. It didn't take Dakota long to figure out who was intercepting those messages. With all her heart she wanted to avoid picking the scab over their semi-argument about Leticia, but she finally had to point out to him that he might be just friends with the woman, but his ex-wife wanted him back.

"Dakota, you're wrong about that. Dead wrong. And even if you were right, I don't want her for anything except a highly efficient office manager which is all that she is," Nick had told her.

"If she's so danged efficient why does she keep losing my messages? That's why I call you on your cell. God help us if you ever lose that, I'd never be able to contact you."

"Baby, you're worried about nothing. Leticia can be a handful, but she ain't stupid. I pay her a good salary and she's not about to jeopardize it by trying some dumb stuff. If I even thought she was trying something crazy she'd be out on her butt and she knows this. Just let it go, Dakota."

And because she trusted Nick with all her heart, she tried her best to do just that.

Dakota and Nick had really managed to compromise on his long working hours. She made the best of the situation she knew how important his work was to him. He'd managed to keep his word and there were very few occasions where he'd had to break a date or reschedule one. The only thing of real importance to her was the black tie affair in October to which he'd promised to escort her.

She was receiving a National Book Award for her latest book, *Blood on the Roses*. It was a fascinating account of murder and mayhem in the elite circles of horse-breeding in Kentucky. She'd worked over a year researching the book and as a result, a person who'd escaped prosecution had been brought to justice. She was understandably proud of her accomplishment and she couldn't wait to have Nick at her side to celebrate.

She had bought an elegant black velvet strapless gown with a matching coat and she looked nothing short of regal in the ensemble. Nick was supposed to have met her at home at five, but he wasn't there. She called his cell phone six times, but he either had it turned off or he wasn't answering. She dallied as long as she could, but when it was apparent that he was going to stand her up, she left. She arrived at the hotel where the gala event was being held just before the cocktail hour ended. Toni came up to her at once, asking where she'd been. "Where's Nick? Parking the car?"

"I have no idea where Nick is," Dakota answered tersely. "I truly hope he has a good excuse for this because I could really hate him right about now."

The banquet went on as scheduled and she received her award with grace and dignity but with no Nick by her side.

Nick was at that very moment cursing up a blue streak. A problem had arisen at one of his work sites about fifty miles from Chicago, and he'd had to check it out himself. It had taken longer than he planned and when he got back to town, it was late. To make matters worse, Lettie was stranded at the office and she had to get home to her kids. Nick had unhesitatingly told her she could use his truck, if she just dropped him at home. "Do me one favor, Lettie. I've got to jump in the shower, so you hold my cell and if Dakota calls tell her I'm on my way. I know I'm running late and I'm sorry, but I'll be there."

"Sure, boss, no problem. You take your time because these things never start on time. If she calls I'll tell her that I'll drop you off at the hotel and you can drive her car home. How's that?" she asked helpfully.

After Dakota had accepted her award she was too upset to linger and she left as soon as possible. She'd called Nick one more time to let him know she was headed to his place and she hoped he had a good explanation for his desertion. When she pulled into the driveway and saw his truck, she was livid. She used her key to let herself in and stormed into the house. In the past few months a sofa and chairs had been added to the living room and that's where she saw the scene that ripped out her heart. Leticia was reclining on the very sofa that she had picked out, wearing only a slip. A glass of wine was at hand and there were candles, her Warm Spirit candles that she'd ordered for Nick, lit everywhere around the room. The CD player was on and the mood was strictly one of seduction. Leticia smiled at her triumphantly.

"If you're looking for Nick he's in the shower. He said I worked him pretty good," she said smugly.

"Give him a message for me, would you? Tell him it's over."

She walked over to where the smirking woman sprawled on the sofa and leaned down. "And can you give him something else, too? Give him this," she said as she drew back her hand and slapped Leticia so hard she rolled off the sofa.

By the time Nick came downstairs, Leticia was fully dressed and looking as innocent as possible under the circumstances. The candles were extinguished and the music was off and she was holding an ice pack to her cheek.

"Lettie, get moving, I'm already late. What the hell are you doing?" Nick demanded.

"I'm icing my cheek where that crazy woman hit me. She came stompin' up in here and cussed me out, then she attacked me," Leticia said tearfully. "What the hell is wrong with her, Nick? I never did anything to her in my life," she added with a pitiful sniff.

"I don't know what the hell is going on here, Lettie, but I've had just about enough of this crap to last me a lifetime. Get the hell out of here and make sure you get my truck back first thing in the morning."

When she hesitated, Nick repeated his words in a louder, rougher tone. "Get out, Lettie, and my truck better be in my driveway come morning."

As brilliantly happy as the summer and fall had been, that's how dreary the rest of the year was for Dakota. When she'd finally tried to make sense of the situation, she knew in her heart that Nick hadn't done anything wrong, it was her insecurity and her jealousy that had done the dirty work. She'd tried to do the right thing and apologize, but it hadn't worked. She took her pride in hand and went to his house a week after the gala and told him to his face that she'd overreacted and she was sorry. "I'm truly sorry, Nick. I saw her lying on our sofa in that cheap slip and I flipped out. I was mad as hell because you hadn't shown up or called me, and I'd been calling you over and over with no answer. Then she stages this phony seduction and I lost it. It was wrong of me and I know it, but I'm hoping we can put it behind us," she said humbly.

She'd never seen his eyes look so cold. She'd never known his eyes could turn so pale and lethal. He let her finish her speech and he said nothing. Finally he said, "I told you, Dakota, when I'm through with something, I'm through. And I'm done with this. If you can't trust me, we have nothing and that's what I'm feeling right now. Not a damned thing."

She couldn't have been more stunned if he'd just slammed the door in her face. What he did was much worse, though—he just walked away and left her in the kitchen to let herself out. She sobbed all the way home and sobbed some more after she got there. That's when she realized how much she really loved Nick. When Jonah had left her she hadn't shed a single tear. Now she avoided everyone, including her own family. Billie had come to visit unexpectedly and was horrified by what she saw. Dakota was down to a size twelve at best, and she looked awful. Her hair was dry and brittle and her skin was blotchy. Billie was ready to kill Nick with her own hands.

She cursed colorfully and eloquently in several languages before she was able to calm down a little. She could see it wasn't making Dakota feel any better and that's all she wanted to do.

"Look, baby sister, I did this. It was all me. I should have popped that hag in the head with a bag of nickels the minute I knew she was after my man, but instead I played right into her little trap. It was all my fault for being insecure and jealous. I was totally irrational. I was pathetic," Dakota admitted. "I just never knew how much I loved him, I guess. I was totally invested in this man to the point I had lost myself in him. I love him completely, Billie, and the thought of him with someone else just about killed me. I've never been involved with anyone to the point where I'd lose my natural mind at the thought of losing him, but here I am. Manless and nuts," she said harshly.

"So what happens now?" Billie asked quietly.

"Nothing. I go on with my life. I went to him and apologized, and he said he was through with me. I even wrote him a letter and it didn't do a particle of good; he never answered it. So, it's over," she said with so much sadness in her voice that Billie wanted to cry.

Dakota saw the look on her sister's beautiful face and hugged her. "It's okay, baby sister. I'll be better tomorrow, I really will. Remember that song, 'Trouble Don't Last Always'? It really doesn't. I might have to leave Chicago, but that's okay. I've had an offer for a new book and a job at the *New York Times*. I'm moving up, Billie. It'll be fine, it really will."

Billie might have believed her sister if she hadn't burst in to wracking sobs at that very moment.

Nick was a miserable man. A miserable man in a really bad mood, the same mood he'd been in since he and Dakota had broken up. Everyone trod lightly around him because *foul* didn't even begin to describe his disposition. He was working harder than ever, but everyone he worked with was on the verge of a nervous collapse. Nick was a kind and understanding person to work for. He wasn't the kind to snap off your head and hand it to you. He was firm, but fair, and he truly cared about developing his employees. Overnight he'd turned into a micromanaging tyrant who flew into rages when things didn't go the way he dictated them.

He was estranged from his family, because Patsy had sided with Dakota. "Nick, I don't mean to be an I-told-you-so, but I told you that keeping that woman on was a mistake. Dakota was right; she's been after you for years, trying to get you back. If you ask me, you need to go over to Dakota's and beg her forgiveness because she was the victim, not the villain."

Nick had snarled at her that he hadn't asked her and he wasn't going to ask her a damned thing. Paul took issue with the way his brother spoke to his wife and the two men who'd never fought in their lives almost came to physical blows. Nick was going downhill fast. When he stopped his twice-weekly washings of his beloved Escalade, even Leticia got nervous.

She was more than nervous, really; she was terrified. She'd gone way too far and she knew it was just a matter of time before the truth came out. It was going to come out one way or another and she wished with all her heart that she had the courage to tell him what she'd done. She might have, if she'd had a little more time on her side, but time wasn't her friend as she discovered one afternoon.

She came into Nick's office to tell him she was leaving for the day and she saw something in his hand that made all the blood in her veins freeze. He was holding a small pink envelope addressed to him and the letter it had contained was on the blotter in front of him. She didn't have long to wait because he lit right into her.

"I had an interesting talk with my mail lady today. I just happened to be leaving the house when she came and she asked me if I'd gotten the letter I was waiting for. Said that my secretary had been to the house several times to get the mail because I was expecting something special. Since you were in the house when she got there, she figured I had sent you. Since I had done nothing of the kind, I thought I'd better do a little investigating and I found this in your desk drawer. Why you were stupid enough to put it there, I'll never know, but I'm glad as hell that you did," he said in a cold, dead voice. "If I hadn't seen it with my own eyes I wouldn't have believed that you were capable of this kind of crap. I thought I knew everything about you, Lettie, the good and the bad, but you surprised even me."

Leticia started stuttering and stammering and trying to explain. "I'm sorry, Nick, I'm sorry. I was wrong, I know I was, but I didn't know what else to do. Your lady wasn't wrong about me, I've been trying to get you back for a long time, but you never noticed. When she came into the picture I knew for sure it was hopeless, but I still had to stick my nose in. The night of that award thing, I didn't need a ride. My car was working just fine. I lied to you so you'd be even later than you were. I turned your phone off so she couldn't get through to you. I erased all the missed calls after she left. I knew she was coming to your house and yeah, I set up a little scene. I don't think she really believed we had done anything, but she was so hurt by then she just had to say something. And after you two broke up I went by your house every day to check your mail because I thought she might write you or something. And when she did, I stole the letter," she admitted. "I'm not lying this time, I really planned to tell you the truth, but I didn't know how to get the words out. I didn't want to lose my job, and I didn't want to lose you, even though I always knew it was hopeless. I knew you'd never take me back. I know how you can be when you're through with something or somebody. But I deserved to be dumped and as far as I can see, Dakota didn't do anything except love you real hard. I'm real sorry about this, Nick. I really am."

"Everybody's sorry about something. And I'm sorry to tell you that I'm giving you three months' severance pay. I don't want to see you here again, Lettie." Nick was leaning back in his big office chair looking utterly exhausted. "Goodbye, Lettie." He stared out the big window to the darkening sky and shook his head. He picked up the letter and read it again, the words searing into his heart like a brand. *Dear Nick,* he read. *It's taken me a long time to finally understand why I behaved the way I did. Nothing has ever meant as much to me as the relationship we shared. In a very short time you became as essential to me as the air I breathe and the intensity of that feeling overwhelmed me. It frightened me as much as it exhilarated me. When you cherish someone or something as much as I did you, the thought of losing that person, that closeness, is more profound than the fear of death. I made a dreadful mistake, one that I'll regret for the rest of my life. But I'll never regret loving you. Always, Dakota.* As soon as he was done with the third reading, he picked up the phone and called the last person on earth who wanted to hear his voice.

Chapter 14

It was early evening when Dakota heard a familiar knock at her door. Her heart jumped and she hesitated before going to the living room to open it. She could see Nick's face in the light that shone outside the door and she hesitated for only a moment before opening the door.

"I tried to call you but you didn't answer the phone," he said gruffly.

Dakota looked at him for a long moment before answering him. "I didn't feel like talking," she said quietly.

"I figured as much, which is why I came over. I got your letter, Dakota. We need to talk," he said in a low voice.

"Talk about what? I sent that letter weeks ago and you're just getting around to wanting to discuss it? That ship has sailed, Nick. This is what they call too little, too late." She brushed her hair away from her face in a weary gesture.

"Can I come in at least? It's kind of hard to talk while I'm standing in the doorway."

She hesitated, her hand tightening on the knob, which she hadn't let go. Cha-Cha came cannoning into the room and went for Nick, which made her decision a moot one. "Come in before she decides to run out," Dakota said impatiently.

Nick scooped up the ecstatic cat and entered the room, walking over to the sofa. "Can I sit down?"

Dakota waved her hand and looked irritated for the first time. "Don't be ridiculous. Sit down," she said with a trace of her usual feistiness.

While Cha-Cha clambered all over her hero with joy, Nick started talking. "Look Dakota, there's a lot we need to discuss. I just read the letter today because I just got it. Lettie had stolen it out of my mailbox when it arrived and I just found it today. I was wrong about a lot of things, but I wasn't wrong to fall in love with you. I want to put this behind us and start over."

Dakota was walking around the living room straightening things that didn't need to be straightened. She finally sat down on the edge of the loveseat and stared at Nick. "I don't think we can, Nick. More importantly, I don't think we should. We fell into a relationship much too quickly. It was like a fire that burned out of control and we both got burned. I invested too much of myself too quickly and that's why I lost my head. I don't want to risk losing my heart again. It's too painful, it's too debilitating. I think we're better off the way we are," she said with a chilling finality.

"So you're just going to give up on me? Just give up on love altogether, is that it? What happened to the woman I met a few months ago? You were a fighter when I met you, baby, what happened to all that backbone?" he demanded. He looked at her intently, taking in every bit of her appearance. She looked worn out, too thin and exhausted and it hurt him to know he was responsible for making her look that way.

She finally answered him with a faint smile. "I learned how to pick my fights better, Nick. I can't do this anymore. I think you should leave."

And because he didn't want to cause her any more distress, he did so, but he had one more thing to say before he walked out the door. "This isn't over, Dakota. Not by a long shot."

Dakota glared at Toni. "Tell me again, how do I let you talk me into these things? The fashion show was bad enough, but this jingle jolly whatever is way over the top, sister."

"It's the Mistletoe Jam and this is not an idea of mine, for once. This is something the paper has sponsored for years and it's customary for everyone to take part in it. It's a nice Christmas show in the old-school tradition and it raises a bunch of money for Children's Hospital. So you'll do it, right?" Toni looked sweet but resolute. There was no point in trying to argue with her anymore.

"All right, all right, all right, all right! I'll do it, but I won't be happy about it. I want that on record," Dakota said grumpily.

It was the week before Thanksgiving and they

were taping the bloody spectacle for airing the day after Thanksgiving or Thanksgiving Day, she didn't know which and didn't care. All she wanted to do was one take, just like Judy Garland did when they shot her singing "Somewhere Over the Rainbow." One take and boom, that was it. Well she was going to hit it in one take tonight or her name wasn't Dakota. Toni had not only coerced her into being in the show, she'd come up with a cockamamie song for her to sing. It was a very jazzy tune called "The Man with the Bag," about Santa coming to town. *Somebody gag me with a big spoon,* she thought. She had to wear an off-the-shoulder red velvet dress with a slit up the side and mistletoe in her freakin' hair. Her only hope of salvation was the thought that her number opened the show and then she could scamper out of there. She wasn't even going to be in the big finale, they had a children's choir for that.

She stood quietly, awaiting her cue. She strolled onto the stage as though she owned it and launched into the complicated riffs with the silly lyrics: Hey, Mr. Kringle, the man with the jingle, blah, blah, blah. She ripped through the song with ease and at the very end she even manage a wink, a smile and a jaunty, "You'd better watch out!" That's when things got crazy. A very tall Santa had appeared at her side and picked her up, throwing her over his shoulder. *Thanks for changing the script, Toni,* she thought as she continued to smile and wave. They could throw anything at her they wanted, she was doing one take and that was it. Santa lumbered off the stage with her, and kept trudging along.

"You can put me down now. Yo, Santa, the take is over, I'm done, put me down. Hey, Kris Kringle, you want to put me down now? Drop me, mister or I'll sue this station for a large sum of money. Where are you taking me, crackpot?"

By now they'd reached the parking lot where a light snow was falling. The runaway Santa had finally set her on her feet and took her upper arms in his gloved hands. "I'll take you to the North Pole if you want me to, but I'd rather take you home," he said.

It was Nick dressed up in that idiotic costume. Nick, the man she'd lost forever.

"Dakota, I owe you an apology. I owe you a lifetime of I'm sorry. I was wrong, baby, I was completely out of line. I was asking you to believe everything I said without hesitation on your part and I wasn't willing to do the same thing for you. I wasn't being fair to you. I know what a low-down liar my ex-wife can be and I should have paid attention to you when you said she was up to something. I got your letter late because she stole it out of my mailbox. I fired her, Dakota. Patsy was right. I should never have kept her on after she got on her feet. *You* were right, she was trying to get with me and I was too stupid to notice. I was as wrong as two left shoes and I need you to forgive me. I need you back in my life, Dakota, because it's been hell without you."

Dakota was too overcome to say anything, something that caused Nick great anguish. "Say something, baby! Even if you tell me to go straight to hell, say something."

Finally, she smiled through the tears that were rolling down her face. "You talk too much," she murmured as she pulled his head down to hers.

She was so engrossed in his kiss she didn't notice the studio's door open. Toni, Billie and Zane were standing there pumping their fists in the air and making all kinds of joyful noise, but Dakota didn't hear a thing.

* * *

Later that night, the two of them were in the living room in front of a roaring fire and the scent of the dozens of roses that filled the solarium. There was a pile of pillows, a mink blanket, Cha-Cha and a big bottle of the most expensive champagne Nick could find. He'd gotten up for a minute and come back with a small velvet box. "Dakota, catch," he said as he tossed the box gently in her direction. She opened it to find a perfect five-carat diamond ring set in platinum. The center stone was a brilliant cut and the high, Tiffany-styled prongs were also studded with diamonds, as was the band. It was like a constellation for her finger. It sparkled like a cluster of stars in the night sky and it was the most beautiful thing she'd ever seen. Nick was at her side at once with a fistful of tissues.

"How about us getting married on Christmas Day? I can't risk you coming to your senses and running off," he said between kisses.

"It sounds perfect. I love you, Nick."

He pulled her into the shelter of his arms and kissed her again. "I love you, Dakota. And nothing is ever coming between us again. I'm going to start delegating more. I want to spend more time with you. I missed you, baby."

"No more than I missed you. You're my other half, Nick."

"And you, Miss Lady, are my heart."

"How did you pull off the Santa coup? That was so sweet. And funny, too," she added as she stared at her ring in the firelight.

"Well, I called Billie and when she got through cussing me out, she got Toni on the phone and we put our heads together. Your boss helped, too. He seems like a pretty cool guy to work for," Nick said as he got more comfortable on the pillows and pulled her into his arms.

"Zane is a pretty cool guy, period. He's crazy about Toni, but she doesn't know it. She's engaged to some macho hockey player and she has no idea Zane adores her."

Nick wasn't really listening to her words, he was enjoying the feel of her against his body too much. "Dakota, I'm serious about getting married on Christmas. I want us to be together as soon as possible for the rest of our lives. I'm making some changes at work, too. I can still get everything done without being there twenty-four seven. It's time for me to quit micromanaging and start letting people do what I pay them to do. And I hired a new office manager, too. I think she's going to work out real well. You're going to like her, I guarantee it."

Dakota was rubbing her cheek against the soft hair on Nick's but she sat up when she heard that. "Don't be so sure of that. As your wife I may demand the right to have final say on this applicant." she said in a mock-stern voice.

"Oh, You'll approve this candidate," he drawled, "Her name is Billie Phillips and she's highly motivated to succeed."

"Billie? I can't wait to hear how this happened," Dakota said with a laugh.

Nick's eyes turned hot and passionate. "You're gonna have to, baby, because right now I don't want to talk about anything. I have better things to do with my mouth, like this here," he said as he took her lips in a long kiss that signaled forever.

Torn between her past and present...

DONNA HILL

ESSENCE BESTSELLING AUTHOR

Elizabeth swore off men after her husband left her for
a younger woman...until sexy contractor Ron Powers
charmed his way into her life. But just as Elizabeth is
embarking on a journey of sensual self-discovery with
Ron, her ex tells her he wants her back. And with Ron's
radical past threatening their future, she's not sure what
to do! So she turns to her "girlz"—Stephanie, Barbara,
Anne Marie and Terri—for advice.

**Pause for Men: Five fabulously fortysomething divas
rewrite the book on romance.**

*Available the first week of July,
wherever books are sold.*

KIMANI™
ROMANCE

www.kimanipress.com

KPDH0240707

He's determined to become the
comeback kid...

THE
VERY
THOUGHT
of
YOU
ANGELA WEAVER

Drafted to hide a witness's daughter in a high-profile
murder case, Department of Justice operative
Miranda Tyler seeks the help of Caleb Blackfox,
who once betrayed her. Now Caleb is willing to do
whatever it takes to win back the girl who got away.

Available the first week of July,
wherever books are sold.

Lights…camera…attraction!

NATIONAL BESTSELLING AUTHOR

SANDRA Kitt

Celluloid Memories

> **Part of Arabesque's sizzling
> Romance in the Spotlight series!**

Savannah Shelton knows the City of Angels breaks hearts
more often than it fulfills dreams. But when a fender bender
introduces her to McCoy Sutton, a charming, sexy attorney,
Savannah wonders if it's time to put aside her jaded ideas
about L.A. and figure out if real life can have
a Hollywood ending….

Available the first week of July wherever books are sold.

ARABESQUE®

www.kimanipress.com

KPSK0150707

Forgiveness takes courage...

A MEASURE OF
Faith

MAXINE BILLINGS

With her loving husband, a beautiful home and two
wonderful children, Lynnette Montgomery feels very
blessed. But a sudden car accident starts a chain of
events that tests her faith, and pulls to the forefront
memories of a very painful childhood. At forty years of
age, Lynnette comes to see that it takes a measure of
faith to help one through the pains of life.

"An enlightening read with an endearing family theme."
—*Romantic Times BOOKreviews*
on *The Breaking Point*

*Available the first week of July
wherever books are sold.*